DEAD IN BED

SWEETFERN HARBOR MYSTERY #2

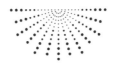

WENDY MEADOWS

MAJESTIC
OWL
PUBLISHING LLC

CHAPTER ONE

THE SEASIDE THEATRE FESTIVAL
COMES TO SWEETFERN HARBOR

*W*hen Shawn Quincy rushed into the sitting room with the news that a cast member of "The Rich Game" had been found dead in bed upstairs, Brenda almost choked on her coffee. As a talented ballet dancer and actor, Shawn had often told stories that made her sides ache with laughter. But Brenda could see by the look on his face that this time his news was real. The owner of the Sheffield Bed and Breakfast quickly set down her coffee and sprinted up the stairs to the room Shawn had pointed out to her.

Breathing hard, Brenda stepped cautiously into the room just long enough to see a body lying unnaturally still atop the quilt. She closed her eyes for a brief moment, then stepped back into the hall.

As she ushered a few curious guests and staff members away and prepared to call the authorities, she realized that the cherished serenity of the Sheffield Bed and Breakfast was about to change.

The Sheffield Bed and Breakfast, a stately, historic Queen Anne-style mansion that boasted gorgeous flower gardens and a sweeping view of the Atlantic Ocean, was a beloved institution in the seaside town of Sweetfern Harbor. Its guests returned year after year, drawn to its charms, but also, perhaps, to its mysteries.

Prior to that fateful morning, Brenda had been enjoying a successful summer season boosted by the notoriety some of her guests had brought with them. The arrival of the stars of the traveling summer theatre festival had been like a free advertisement for the bed and breakfast. The Seaside Theatre Festival was a famous summer event that toured up and down the Atlantic coast each year, performing a new play in town theatres and even outdoor parks. It had been a major coup that the festival had not only picked Sweetfern Harbor as a stop on their tour this year, but even better – the Sheffield Bed and Breakfast would be where the actors would stay.

Word spread throughout Sweetfern Harbor like wildfire before their arrival. The well-known actress Ellen Teague was to feature as the star of the festival's play.

Another big draw was the young and devastatingly handsome actor Shawn Quincy, who drew younger crowds that swooned like Elvis fans of an earlier era. There was also Anna Quincy, Shawn's young and talented wife, the acclaimed comedian Ricky Owens, and the young ingénue Bonnie Ross in her first role.

When Brenda received the phone call informing her about this prestigious booking, she had stood in shock looking at the list of names in her hand. Now that it was the day of their arrival, she found herself gazing at the list again.

"Are you nervous?" asked Allie. The sixteen-year-old beamed. Allie was her office manager when not in school. "I mean, it's really something that Ellen Teague will actually sleep in one of the beds upstairs." She breathed deeply and visibly swooned. "I have to say my favorite is that good-looking Shawn Quincy. Have you ever seen him dance? I'd love just one dance with him someday. I can only imagine his arms around me."

Brenda laughed fondly at the starstruck look in Allie's eyes. "Who knows? You may get your chance. Though I should remind you that he's married. I know Anna plays his wife in the show, too." Brenda paused and then answered Allie's question. "I guess I am a little nervous...but it's because I've always been a huge fan of Ellen Teague. I wonder what she's really like in person."

It was going to be a big weekend and everyone at

Sheffield Bed and Breakfast scurried around to make things perfect. Brenda glanced through the wide sitting room window. In approximately one hour, the cast of the hit play "The Rich Game" would arrive.

As Brenda watched, Jenny Rivers parked in front, then jumped out to swing open the back door of her van. The florist unloaded an armful of beautiful floral arrangements.

"I have them all here, Brenda." Jenny elbowed the front door open and Brenda took the large vase from her, inhaling the sweet perfume of the arrangement. "I'll be bringing a lot more before this weekend is over. I'm already doing a booming business because of the theatre festival and your special guests."

"This is beautiful. I can always count on quality from you, Jenny. I'm glad this helps your business, too. Every shop on Main Street should have a good weekend."

"Are they here yet?" Jenny looked around the front hall of the bed and breakfast, her eyes wide with curiosity.

Brenda shook her head. "No, but they'll be here soon." Jenny's crestfallen face told her that the young florist, too, wanted to get a firsthand look at the prestigious guests. "Don't worry. You'll get to meet them all. Their first performance is tomorrow."

Jenny sighed. "I know, but I hoped I came at the right

time to see them check in. I have a few more vases in the car. Where do you want them?"

Brenda gave her instructions and Jenny offered to complete the arrangements by setting them up. Her talent was not just making beautiful bouquets, but choosing the perfect settings for them.

"If you want to, we can take the large spray of roses and dahlias up to Ellen Teague's quarters," Brenda offered. She delighted to see Jenny's reaction.

"I'd love to see where she is staying," said Jenny, fighting to refrain from gushing. She carried the large bouquet up to the suite reserved for the star. When Brenda unlocked the door, Jenny stepped inside and walked slowly around the spacious room that included a large walk-in closet with a dressing table.

"I gave her this room because the extra closet will hold all the costumes, and the dressing table is perfect for makeup. It was something she specifically asked for."

"Everything is just beautiful, Brenda." The florist gazed around the room, which had been polished and shined within an inch of its life.

Brenda was pleased that Jenny liked it so much. Allie had helped her brainstorm a few extra special finishing touches. The rich Belgian chocolates perched on the lace pillow sham and bottle of Moët and Chandon Champagne on the antique bureau with crystal champagne glasses would be enough to tempt anyone. She double-checked that the bathroom was impeccably clean and stocked with fresh, fluffy towels.

"Allie even had the idea to email Ellen's assistant and ask her what kinds of books she likes to read," said Brenda proudly, glancing at the small array of classics in several genres posed on the bedside console. A variety of movies had been added to the console as well, and an assortment of music, which included a couple of operas.

Jenny gazed around the room in awe at the attention to detail. "I suppose you know Ellen Teague has won five Oscars and two Tony awards for her acting," said Brenda.

"And she's a famous director, too," added Jenny, adjusting the vase carefully where she had set it on an antique lace doily so it was reflected in the bureau mirror. Brenda nodded in admiration. There was little she did not know about Ellen Teague. Brenda found the woman fascinating. She lived a glamorous life that led Brenda's imagination in wild directions.

"Do you have time to show me where everyone else will stay?"

Brenda showed her the way to a smaller, tasteful room immediately next to Ellen's, which was to be for her personal assistant. "This room has access to Ellen's. It's for her assistant, Chester Boyd. I understand he makes all arrangements for her and is responsible for all the show's particulars. He also makes sure Ellen is comfortable and prepared."

They crossed the wide planked hallway to view the room where Shawn and Anna Quincy would stay and Jenny admired the stunning view of the cascading rose arbors in the garden below. After showing Jenny where everyone would be staying, Brenda turned to point out two doors at the far end of the hall.

"Those two are lucky, they are the only guests here who are not with the Seaside Theatre Festival. They are regulars here and come twice a year in the summer and in the winter. When I told them in confidence, they insisted they did not expect to get their usual quarters. I think they are thrilled to be here at the same time the performers are."

Just then, they heard voices downstairs and turned to look at each other in realization of who it must be. Brenda smiled at Jenny and said, "Here's your chance. If you want to see the cast firsthand, follow me." In her excitement, Jenny nearly tripped on the top step. Brenda reached out a hand to steady her and together they descended the staircase. As they reached the first floor, they heard the actors practically bubbling with excitement as they exclaimed over the beautiful décor of the Sheffield house. Brenda gestured for Jenny to wait to one side while she greeted her famous guests. It was going to be a perfect weekend at the bed and breakfast.

Brenda couldn't help but look behind everyone to search for her favorite star.

"If you are looking for Ellen, she is following us in her limousine. Chester is with her." Anna Quincy stepped toward Brenda and introduced herself. Brenda had seen Anna in a few movies and was not surprised to see that she was even more beautiful in person. Anna introduced her to everyone else, and Brenda tried to suppress the nervous flutter in her stomach as she shook the hands of these stars who had just stepped into her bed and breakfast.

When Brenda had everyone's attention, she gave them a warm welcome and passed out the room keys. The guests were shown to their rooms on the second floor, not far from the suite waiting for Ellen Teague.

"I hope everything meets your expectations," said Allie, hovering at Brenda's elbow as she watched Shawn open the door of the room for his young wife. Brenda pointed out Chester's and Ellen's rooms to Anna. "We felt this would serve their purposes, since he is her assistant. Also, there is plenty of room for costumes and makeup in her room."

"Are we the only ones booked this weekend?" asked Bonnie, who tucked one curling tress behind her ear as she stood in the doorway of her room.

"We have two other guests who always come this

weekend every year, but they are separate from your group at the far end. You can see where the hallway turns a little. They are down there."

"This place must have a lot of nooks and crannies…or maybe crooks and nannies," said Ricky, cracking a smile, "and plenty of stories to tell."

"It has a ton of history," Allie piped up eagerly, seeming to enjoy the moment when everyone's eyes landed on her. Brenda watched her young employee with amusement as she continued to tell them a portion of the old house's history with enthusiasm.

Before Allie could bore their guests, Brenda gently interrupted her to invite them all for refreshments. "The sitting room is just across from the front entrance. Our tea and pastries are famous, so I hope I'll see you downstairs."

When Brenda returned to the foyer, she found Jenny standing with her eyes wide and sparkling, watching as the entourage descended the stairs. As much as Jenny clearly wanted to linger, she excused herself with an excited smile at Brenda and then left to return to her shop.

In the sitting room, the housekeeper Phyllis Lindsey had laid a sumptuous spread of delicate pastries, fruit, and other treats, with a beautiful antique teapot and china teacups at the ready. The actors were charmed to meet the capable Phyllis and exclaimed at her excellent tea, and as they sat to eat their refreshments, the conversations were lively.

Bonnie Ross laughed easily and enjoyed everyone around her. Her curly auburn hair and warm demeanor seemed to spread a glow over every movement she made. When Brenda asked her role in the play, she smiled broadly.

"I'm rather new to this but have been cast in the role of the young hostess of the country estate where the play takes place. It's not a big part but it sure made me happy when I was cast for it. It's my first big break."

Brenda congratulated her. "My wife and I play the married couple," Shawn Quincy chimed in. "Do you know the play?" Brenda nodded, having read a brief description of "The Rich Game" in the local newspaper.

"And my role is the lowly husband of our luminous star," said Ricky Owens. The fortyish looking man tilted his head and humor was evident in his blue eyes. He stroked his beard as if by habit.

"I have heard of you," said Phyllis as she refilled Ricky's teacup. "You have won many awards."

"I'd say his biggest role is pretending to be Ellen's husband," said Shawn with dry humor. "I'm sure you have to agree with that, Ricky."

Ricky rolled his eyes. "I've managed."

Brenda picked up a vibe she couldn't put her finger on. The actors seemed at ease with one another, but they conveyed something more without words. Before she could ask a question, Allie jumped up at the sound of a limousine pulling up in front of the bed and breakfast. All eyes turned to look at the open doorway that led to the check-in counter. No one spoke and Brenda leapt to her feet with excitement.

But when she reached the foyer, her enthusiastic welcome for Ellen Teague faded a little when she saw that the much-admired star stood coldly before her and barely returned her greeting. Her idol stood before her in a pale green silk dress, tasteful heels, and a wide-brimmed hat. It was a strange contrast to the amiable and relaxed scene she had just exited.

A man stepped toward Brenda and extended his hand. "I am Chester Boyd, and this is Miss Teague," he said, shaking her hand formally.

Brenda had been expecting a young assistant, but Chester reminded her more of a butler. His perfectly coiffed dark hair held tinges of grey. His stance was erect and his attention was focused entirely on Ellen Teague.

"I presume Miss Teague's quarters are ready for her?" His arched eyebrows indicated a demand rather than a question.

"Of course, please follow me."

When Brenda turned to lead them upstairs, she caught a glimpse of the coal black hair and pale skin of Ellen Teague. She knew the woman was younger than her own forty-six years, but right now the star looked ten years older than Brenda. And that famous face she had seen so many times on the screen looked different. Under the brim of her hat, her dark eyes were outlined with heavy makeup.

Ellen surveyed the foyer from top to bottom, prompting Brenda to wait at the foot of the stairs. So far, her idol had not spoken. Brenda tried to chalk the aloof manner up to the tiresome drive to Sweetfern Harbor, even though it wasn't that far from New York City. Brenda waited for the next move.

At last, Ellen Teague turned toward the staircase, and Chester followed close behind her. When she opened the door, Brenda held her breath while the actress walked slowly around the suite. In the sunlight that fell through the lace curtains, a sapphire ring gleamed on Ellen's slender finger and caught Brenda's eye. She noted that it matched her earrings and necklace. The silk dress Ellen wore was from Versace. Brenda recognized the design instantly since she had dreamed about owning one just like it ever since seeing it on the cover of Vogue magazine. Ellen lifted the large-brimmed hat from her head and Chester stepped forward in time to take it from her. At last, she spoke.

"Every costume must be dry-cleaned and pressed before our opening night tomorrow. I take it that is one of your duties?"

"I have someone who can take care of that right away for you, I know the owner of the dry-cleaner here in town. I am the owner of the bed and breakfast and I have very capable staff who will take care of that for you."

Ellen sniffed and her eyes ran over Brenda as if assessing her dress code as owner of the establishment. "That will be all."

Chester followed Brenda into the hallway. "You will have to excuse Miss Teague. She has had a trying last few days rehearsing and preparing for the performances this weekend."

Brenda smiled and assured him she understood. As she walked back downstairs, she tried to imagine the glitz and glamor of the life of a star – but also the work and the demanding schedule. She hoped the arrogant attitude Ellen displayed was indeed due to stress and fatigue, and was not her usual demeanor. Every time she had seen her in movies, Brenda had come away with an impression of her as a strong but ultimately warm woman, someone with tremendous depth and feeling. Surely it was not all an act.

When she entered the sitting room, the atmosphere was noticeably subdued. Anna whispered something to her husband and Shawn nodded in agreement. Even Ricky Owens appeared lost in his thoughts as he gazed out the window, his eyes fixated on the side lawn and gardens of Sheffield Bed and Breakfast. Brenda glanced at young Bonnie Ross and caught her eye with a questioning glance. Bonnie answered her with only a lopsided grin and then excused herself from the room.

Allie saved the day when she bounded into the room to offer a tour of the grounds. Her sudden interruption was like a breath of fresh air in the room, and the actors happily followed her outside, more than ready to take in the salt breeze and the lush gardens and leave the strange hush of the sitting room behind.

CHAPTER TWO

A NIGHT OUT

*B*renda headed up to her apartment for a much-needed break after getting her guests settled in. Halfway up the stairs, she greeted Chester on his way down. He bowed slightly and stopped at the landing where a stained-glass window filtered prettily colored light onto a velvet-cushioned window seat.

"I looked at the books in Miss Teague's room. Are they first editions as requested?"

"I am not sure. A few may be." In fact, Brenda had not thought to ask Allie if there had been such specific instructions in the email.

"Please check, since I was quite specific. Miss Teague refuses to read anything except first editions."

Brenda stared at him. Chester returned her look

wordlessly. He then turned and walked back up the stairs just as his boss called his name. Evidently, Ellen Teague demanded his services. Brenda hoped Ellen would get a good night's sleep so as to awaken in a better mood the next day. Without even going to her apartment, she turned to go back downstairs and down the narrow passageway to the kitchen. She was determined to make sure that the dinner menu was scrutinized and every detail perfected. Together with the chef, she carefully reviewed the menu and they discussed every request from Ellen, who had sent additional requests regarding the evening meal.

"Add more variety to the side dishes with the entrée in case the others don't like what she has ordered for the table," Brenda said, fretting as she surveyed everything in preparation stages laid out in the kitchen.

"I will do everything to keep all guests satisfied during the evening meal, Brenda." Her chef, Morgan, a talented woman in her mid-fifties, was always her rock in the storm, and had weathered Brenda's nerves many times. She gave her boss a patient smile.

Brenda patted Morgan's arm in thanks and reminded herself that her chef's culinary skills were renowned for a reason. Allie was next on her list. She found her trooping back into the house through the rear hallway with the cast members, who thanked the young girl and headed up to their rooms. Brenda told Allie of Chester's inquiry regarding the first editions.

"Is there a difference? I got her a bunch of beautiful copies of classics, like her assistant said."

"No, first editions are when a book was printed for the first time. The classics especially are in high demand if they are first editions – they can fetch thousands of dollars and be collector's items." Brenda shook her head. "Apparently, she likes her new books to be first editions, too. She is a particular woman, it seems. Will you please look in our library and try to find some first editions? I know my uncle had a number of them in there."

"I'll look for some. How do I know if they are the right ones?"

"They'll only have one year listed on the publication page. Find whatever you can and I'll run the titles past Chester." Brenda sighed as they walked to the library. Her perfect weekend was off to a rocky start.

Allie hesitated with her hand on the doorknob of the library. "The rest of the cast kept making remarks about her. I don't think they like her much."

"It may prove to be a long weekend," said Brenda, "but we'll get through it. Let's just try to keep this kind of gossip under wraps – I would be mortified if she found out the staff was talking about her like this." Allie nodded somberly and Brenda hoped her young employee would take the admonishment to heart. She changed the topic. "You know, I'm really looking forward to seeing 'The Rich Game.' I hear it got rave reviews in New York."

The teenager stepped into the library and gazed out the window, which looked out across the lawn to the street. Suddenly her eyes lit up. "Never mind the play...don't you have a date tonight with Mac?"

Brenda caught her breath and followed Allie's glance to see a familiar car pull up to the curb. "I had no idea it was this late. We're supposed to go down to the Italian café that just opened on Main Street." Allie grinned at her.

Brenda hurried to a small mahogany-framed mirror that hung on the wall of the library and smoothed down her hair, feeling a fluttering sensation like a butterfly in her stomach.

The door to the foyer opened and she stepped into the hall to greet the handsome Detective Mac Rivers. He gave Brenda a warm, meaningful look that made her heart skip a beat. He bent and kissed her lightly.

"I suppose your celebrities made it in okay." The masculine timbre of his voice suddenly reminded her that a date was more interesting than dealing with Ellen Teague.

Brenda glanced at her watch impatiently. "They'll be down for dinner in a few minutes. I'll just welcome them to the table and then I'll freshen up and be ready in no time. I'm excited to try out that new café."

She had already asked Allie and Phyllis to take charge of serving dinner. Brenda crossed her fingers hoping there wouldn't be any glitches, but she knew she was lucky to have such a responsible and reliable staff to step in for her.

Brenda changed for her date and came back down to greet Mac again. "I'm so glad to see you, but I don't want to take longer than an hour and a half away, especially tonight," said Brenda, glancing worriedly toward the closed door of the dining room.

"You seem a little nervous. Is it because your favorite star Ellen Teague is here?" he teased.

"She's actually rather demanding and I'm worried that we got off to a bad start. But I trust Allie and Phyllis. And you know, Phyllis has an uncanny sense of intuition for certain things." She laughed. "I think she will foresee any demands Ellen will have before they come to a head."

"Then let's go and try out that Italian food." His eyes lit up with a special warmth and Brenda wondered what he was planning. "I have something special for you tonight after dinner." When they got to his car, he reached inside and handed her a bouquet of wildflowers. "These are for you, but they are only a teaser. Jenny told me you always love the wildflowers when they arrive at her shop."

Brenda took the gorgeous bouquet and smelled the delicate blooms, which looked like they had been plucked from a mountain meadow.

"Your daughter knows me well. They are beautiful. Thank you." She looked from her flowers up to the night sky and felt the gentle evening breeze on her skin. "Let's leave the bouquet in the car until after dinner and walk down to the café."

"I like that idea." He took her arm and his closeness sent shivers down her spine as they walked together into town.

She admired the detective in many ways. Not only was he good at his job but he was the perfect gentleman when it came to courting a woman. She couldn't help but feel safe and cherished and ladylike when he was around, and it was a pleasure to go for a simple walk down the sidewalk on the arm of such a handsome man.

They came to the café with its intimate lighting and cozy tables and Brenda thought she had never seen something so enticing in her life. Mac pulled out her chair when they approached a corner table. Their server lit the candle in the center and handed them menus. Aromas drifted into the dining room every time a server came and went from the kitchen. The night promised to be a perfect one, except Brenda couldn't get Ellen off her mind.

Mac could tell she was still troubled, and so he asked her more about what happened. She attempted to describe the star to Mac. She told him of her rudeness and repeated the story about the first editions.

"Maybe she gets like that before a performance. I've heard it's common for show people to be on edge before a big performance night," said Mac. "It could be her mental status is on the brink hoping things go as well as they did in New York. The town is overflowing with tourists who are here mainly to see her perform." Mac smiled at her. "Just give her a chance. I'm sure things will be a whole lot different tomorrow."

His logic made sense to her and Brenda realized she had overreacted. "I'm sure you're right. I've always admired her and have seen every movie she ever made – I shouldn't have placed such high expectations on her, perhaps."

When the Caesar salads arrived at their table, Mac told her a funny story of something that happened with his boss at work. Police Chief Bob Ingram was a serious man and plain spoken. The story revolved around a long spiel the chief gave a prisoner's wife about the necessity of searching her before the visit. He turned her over to an officer nearby and then was flabbergasted when the officer struggled to keep a smile off her face. Then the young officer explained the woman didn't know a word of English.

The story was humorous and Mac was a great storyteller but Brenda knew she laughed harder than it deserved. The relief she felt at not being near Ellen Teague right now was something that surprised her. Mac had assessed it all correctly and she hoped she managed to shake the star from her mind for the rest of the evening. Ellen Teague simply needed a good night's sleep. And Brenda Sheffield needed a good night out.

"Now that you've loosened up, let's finish this meal and get some fresh air." He picked up his fork. "I've been waiting for months to try this place out. Did I tell you I lived in Italy for a year? It was back in college, but I've never forgotten how much I liked their food."

"I still have a lot to learn about you, Mac Rivers." Brenda smiled to herself, picturing a young Mac strolling through the streets of an Italian village. She dug into her linguine in clam sauce with gusto and he did the same with his fettuccine alfredo.

As they finished dinner, Brenda's curiosity about his surprise returned. "Mac, I'm too curious...let's skip dessert," she said. Mac chuckled. In the glimmer of the candlelit restaurant, the combination of his blonde hair and startling blue eyes gave him a boyish look. He was a few years younger than she was, but the slight age difference didn't deter the mutual attraction that was like an electrified connection between them.

One thing he loved about Brenda was her insatiable

curiosity. She was like a child waiting for Christmas morning. He loved indulging her, so he declined dessert as well and paid the bill.

Once outside, he drew her away from the wide windows of the café toward the wide sweep of the Atlantic Ocean and took her gently into his arms as they watched the glimmer of the moon on the water. Then he stepped back and pulled a tiny velveteen box from his pocket. Her eyes opened wide as she turned to watch him.

"Brenda, since the day you arrived here I have loved you." He opened the box and she saw a delicate, sparkling ring. On closer observation, it didn't look like an engagement ring. She wasn't quite ready for a step like that anyway, and waited with bated breath for his next words. "This is not an engagement ring. At least, not yet. This is my promise of love for you. I want to develop a deeper love and friendship and learn all I can about you. This is a promise ring for you that hopefully will bring us together, even closer than we are now. I hope you will accept it in the same spirit I offer it to you."

Her relief spilled out. "I love the idea of a promise ring. It is a step forward for us. Thank you, Mac. I accept." She stepped closer to him, looking deeply in his eyes, and he reached out to take her hand in his.

He slipped the ring onto her finger. His arms enfolded her again and he drew her close. People coming and going from the restaurant looked their way and smiled.

Brenda released a happy sigh and stepped back from the embrace to smile back. Then she turned to Mac, realizing what came next. There was a catch in her voice she tried to control. "We'd better get moving," she said.

"I don't want our night to be over so soon, but you're right. It's a big weekend for you."

They walked back to Sheffield Bed and Breakfast, her arm tucked under his. Brenda felt the promise ring gleaming on her finger with happiness and hope, but she turned her mind resolutely toward her duties. When they reached the Sheffield, lights blazed from nearly every room, spilling out across the lawn in the darkness. Brenda silently thanked her Uncle Randolph Sheffield for leaving the Queen Anne-style mansion establishment to her. She had met him only once as a very young child but had never forgotten his kindness to her. In memory of that kindness, she vowed that she would not be deterred by her guest's cold demeanor.

"It looks like everything is still standing" she said, realizing she was stalling. She gazed at the wide front porch that wrapped around the house to one side where several sturdy antique rocking chairs sat vacant. "Oh, let's not go inside yet." She led him around to the privacy of the backyard where the rose arbors trailed down the garden's edge and the view of the sea. They sat down in the Adirondack chairs and listened to the waves that lapped against the rocks. Far in the distance they could see the lights of a large ship far out at sea. "I once thought of replacing the paintings throughout the bed and breakfast. Did you know that?"

"I didn't know that, but I'm glad you didn't. Randolph was very proud of his collection of nautical paintings. Those old ships are stunning."

Brenda laughed softly. "I've gotten used to them. Though sometimes, on a night like tonight, it makes me wish I could jump into one of those old paintings and sail away to sea. Just like in the old days."

Mac reached for her hand and clasped it in his. They sat in silence. Breathing in the salt air enhanced their senses. Every smell and sound under the star-studded night sky held them both spellbound. Brenda wordlessly said a prayer of thanks for her wonderful life and for the man sitting next to her.

"I hate to give this up, but I should get back inside and check on things. The cast will be out most of tomorrow for rehearsals before the first performance tomorrow night."

"I'll pick you up early enough for the play. I hope I'm not too late to get tickets. I hear they are selling out fast."

"I didn't realize you hadn't gotten the tickets yet. If they are sold out we can go the second night."

She tried to hide her disappointment. She knew Mac was

busy at the police station and she had not thought about tickets. Preparing her staff and the bed and breakfast for the guests had consumed her energies.

"I'll make it work somehow, Brenda. I just let that slip up on me. I'm sorry."

"Don't worry about it. We'll see it soon enough. If we miss getting tickets for the first performance I'm sure there are tickets for the second one still available. If we miss tomorrow night it will give us more time together, just the two of us."

Mac's mouth curved in a slow smile. "I like that idea."

After retrieving her flowers from Mac's car and kissing him goodnight, she went into the bed and breakfast. Allie met her at the door and gushed about the dinner, which had been praised as delicious by all the actors – except Ellen.

"Ellen ate very little and left the table midway through the meal. We couldn't tell if it was the food or if she just wasn't hungry." Brenda caught her breath to hear this. "Really, things went fine, Brenda," Allie reassured her. She followed Brenda to the kitchen where she retrieved a vase for her flowers. "And Chester followed her upstairs. Everyone else stayed and enjoyed the food and drinks later. Shawn told us not to worry, Ellen does that often."

"Did she complain about the food?"

Allie shook her head. "Nope. She just left and Chester followed her. Phyllis went up later and asked her if she wanted a hot dinner or dessert or a snack brought up to her room. Ellen declined but Phyllis thought Chester might want to eat something. So she left a covered hot dinner outside his room. She put it in a warmer so it would stay hot." Brenda was gratified to hear that Phyllis's gift of intuition had once again provided a special touch for their guests.

"Perhaps Ellen will be in a better mood tomorrow after she's had a good night's sleep," Brenda commented.

"I'm not so sure about that. Even Ricky Owens made a snide remark about her after she left, and he wasn't joking this time."

"Allie, remember these are our guests. My uncle would have said they deserve kind treatment no matter what we may overhear, remember that. Let's just see what tomorrow brings. Thank you for doing a good job tonight. I'll go see Phyllis now. Goodnight."

When she knocked on Phyllis's door, the fiftyish woman opened it with a smile. When Brenda walked in, she saw William Pendleton sitting in an armchair with a glass of wine in his hand.

"I'm sorry. I didn't realize you were here, William." She turned to Phyllis. "I'll see you in the morning before breakfast. I mainly wanted to thank you for taking over tonight. Allie told me of your thoughtfulness toward Chester. I'm sure he was quite hungry for something."

William waved his hand. "There's no need for an apology. I'll be leaving now."

"You stay right where you are, William," said Phyllis. "There are no secrets between us and unless Brenda is reluctant to speak in front of you it is fine that you listen in." Phyllis looked at Brenda questioningly.

"I have no problem if he hears. I just wanted to ask if you knew why Ellen didn't stay for dinner." Brenda inquired about the menu and the email with its many requests, hoping there had not been some detail amiss.

Phyllis spread her hands open. "She just up and left without saying anything really. Chester followed her out and no one said anything until they were out of earshot. Several people made cutting remarks about it but no one dwelled on the matter. It helped when she left since everyone loosened up and enjoyed the meal."

"I think the weight of her responsibilities is taking its toll on her. After all, it's just before an important performance and a lot depends on her."

"It is Ellen's way," said William. "She can be uptight at times." He laughed as the two women swiveled to look at him in surprised curiosity. "Yes, I know her somewhat. I had a hand in persuading the theatre festival to come here."

They chatted briefly about Ellen as William explained how they had met at a long-ago party when Ellen had been just a young Broadway star and William had worked in New York City. Over the years they had met many times, and he had followed her career avidly, even donating to support the Seaside Theatre Festival. Despite her curiosity, Brenda could tell the couple were eager to get back to their glasses of wine, and she soon bid them goodnight.

On her way to her apartment on the second floor, she took a side stairway, hoping not to run into anyone. She thought about how William and Phyllis had found true love later in life. They were compatible and she was sure they would tie the knot soon. William Pendleton was a very wealthy man, having inherited the vast holdings his wife had hoarded before her untimely death. He was kind and devoted to every person in the tight-knit seaside town of Sweetfern Harbor. She felt sure Phyllis would leave Sheffield Bed and Breakfast once she married William, despite her housekeeper's dedication to the bed and breakfast and indebtedness to Brenda's late Uncle Randolph Sheffield. Whether Phyllis stayed or departed, Brenda found herself smiling at the thought of her as William's future wife.

As she approached her apartment door, Brenda turned when she heard Chester Boyd's voice.

"Ms. Sheffield. I meant to deliver these to you earlier but

your housekeeper told me you were out for a while." He handed her two tickets to the first performance of the play.

But before Brenda could reply, she heard Ellen Teague call to him from her room, in an imperious voice. He nodded in response to Brenda's hurried thanks as he turned on his heel to go.

Brenda felt overjoyed at this stroke of luck and felt that perhaps Uncle Randolph was watching over her. She quickly opened the door to her suite of rooms and called Mac to give him the good news.

CHAPTER THREE

THE PERFORMANCE

*E*arly the next morning, Chester approached Brenda again just as she was entering the dining room for breakfast.

"Miss Teague has requested to use the back lawn for the final rehearsal. I hope this is not a great inconvenience for you."

Brenda froze in the doorway and took in the cool look in Chester's eyes. She had not expected this but was determined to make the best of it for her famous guests. "Of course, we would be happy to have it here. What time will she expect things to be ready?"

"The cast will be in costume by ten this morning. She does not want this advertised, so please advise your staff to be discreet. There will be no 'fans' admitted to the rehearsal." He gave this last command with an air of disapproval and finality, glancing at Allie as she walked past them into the dining room. "But if the staff is free, they are welcome to watch," he finished.

Brenda was both pleasantly surprised at this offer and anxious to know what arrangements would need to be made for scenery or props. Chester waved her concerns aside. "You do not have to worry about any of that. The particulars have been arranged. The costumes are back from the dry-cleaners and everything is ready."

Brenda thanked Chester and as she ate a hasty breakfast, made a mental note to give her staff a bonus when the weekend was over and the cast had departed from the bed and breakfast. This was turning into a much different weekend than she had at first envisioned. Ten minutes later, she gathered everyone in the kitchen with the chef to tell them of the developments. Although Morgan was already busy with preparations for dinner, Brenda asked her to make fresh lemonade to be served on the lawn as refreshments for the actors. Allie offered to step in to bake cookies and Phyllis offered to make a tray of sandwiches to be set out, and the chef nodded her thanks to both of them.

Since there were still a couple hours before the rehearsal was due to begin, Brenda directed Phyllis to first clean any of the vacated rooms to get a head start. "Anyone who has gone to put on their costume and get into makeup – start with their rooms. Leave Ellen's suite until the rehearsal begins. In between times you can help down here with the food. Thank you, all of you. Please remember we have been invited to watch the rehearsal but we must be discreet. Ellen doesn't want word to get around town and I'd hate to see the look on Chester's face if some tourists appeared in the garden. If we can, let's watch out for any stragglers and try to redirect them before they try walking around to the back garden today, okay?"

Brenda planned to supervise and especially ensure no unwanted guests wandered through the rehearsal, but secretly she was thrilled to be immersed in the theatre world. Her interest in Hollywood, Broadway and all things show business peaked now that it was literally at her doorstep. She stood on the lawn and watched as the final preparations were made. The cast members, transformed into their characters with the aid of sumptuous costumes and expert stage makeup, stood waiting for Ellen Teague. Though she was the star, she was also the director.

When Ellen finally appeared on the lawn and called out, "Places!" to her fellow actors to start the show, Brenda could practically see the tension in the air. For it seemed that Ellen Teague's mood had not improved overnight. The bright sunny day with soft ocean breezes didn't improve it, either. Brenda held her breath watching the star command the other actors with only a few subtle words, or an imperious shake of her head. She demanded perfection, and as the rehearsal wore on, she had the actors run through certain scenes over and over again as she focused on errors that Brenda could not even discern from the audience. Even though it was supposed to be a comedy, the smallest infraction was elevated to something that would either make or break the entire performance according to Ellen.

After two hours of rehearsal, the sun was high in the sky when Allie rolled a large cart onto the lawn with platters of sandwiches, lemonade and iced tea. Ellen broke her focus from the scene to glance at the long table and announced a break.

Brenda was relieved on behalf of the actors, several of whom seemed to be sweating slightly in their costumes. She went to the end of the table to help Allie arrange the cookies on a large platter and to pour drinks for the weary actors.

If Brenda had been hoping to talk to her idol over lunch, she had to quickly swallow her disappointment. She watched out of the corner of her eye as Ellen spoke briefly to Chester, then went to sit some distance away at a small table under an elm tree. Chester filled a plate for her and carried it over to her, returning for his own plate and their drinks. Brenda resolved to not let Ellen spoil her day, so when she sat down with her own sandwich, she started a conversation with Anna Quincy.

"I loved you in that scene just now. How long have you been an actress?"

"Not long, actually. I have been a ballet dancer since I was quite young – that's how I met Shawn. He was older than I but every time his class got a break, he used to watch my classes through the studio windows." She smiled at the memory. "He later went on to Broadway and performed in many shows as a dancer, and then started auditioning for acting roles as well. On Broadway, if you're a dancer you practically have to be an actor, too! By that time, I became an understudy for the same shows."

"How did you get this role?"

Shawn joined his wife, setting down a cup of iced tea before her. "Don't let her fool you...there are a couple of minor dance scenes in 'The Rich Game,' but we both auditioned for this one because we wanted speaking roles for a change. We think it is rejuvenating to try something different once in a while. This is Anna's first big role." Adoration filled his eyes as he gazed at his beautiful young wife.

Ricky Owens joined them. Brenda was getting a feel for how the actors all seemed to be so friendly with each other that they naturally gravitated to each other for conversation – all except Ellen, of course. She had to laugh at her train of thought because at that very moment, young Bonnie walked up balancing her plate and drink and pouted prettily at the lack of chairs to join them, and someone immediately suggested they all move to the longer picnic table set up on the small flagstone patio on one side of the garden. With a dimpled grin, Bonnie insisted that Brenda join them. Brenda happily grabbed her sandwich and drink and followed the cast.

"Sheffield Bed and Breakfast is just wonderful. Like a place from another time. It's strange though not to see Randolph around. We all miss him," said Ricky. Brenda turned to regard him with surprise. "If you ever wanted to watch a real actor it would have been Randolph Sheffield."

"That's to say nothing of his directing talent," said Anna.

Brenda was speechless. The others chimed in and couldn't say enough about their time working with her uncle on stage.

"I never knew he was in show business," she said. Then it was their turn to stare at her in amazement.

"He was so talented," said Ricky. "How did you not know this about him?"

"I guess I'm wondering that myself, too. I didn't know him well at all. My parents spoke of him on occasion but I never once heard them say anything about a career in show business. We lived in Michigan and only visited once when I was a young child. And I knew that later he retired and turned the house into a bed and breakfast, but I guess I never knew what he had retired from."

"Anna and I worked with him often but didn't know him as well as Ricky and Ellen did. He wasn't just good on stage – he was always so generous and kind to everyone," said Shawn. "Wasn't Chester a good friend of his, too, before he started working for Ellen?" He turned to Ricky for verification.

"Yes, they were very good friends. Chester was a great admirer of Randolph's, too. As I recall, Randolph had already inherited a fortune when he was young – he decided to get into acting and directing because it was his passion, not because it made him a star. Anyway, I'm surprised no one mentioned this before. We loved Randolph so much, that's why we just had to come to Sweetfern Harbor for the touring theatre festival and stay in the bed and breakfast that was his home and business for so many years. I think he is the one who convinced the Seaside Theatre Festival to come here in the first place."

Bonnie seemed to take in Brenda's pensive look and laid a gentle hand on her arm. "Although I never met your uncle, I have heard a lot about him. He was a role model for many young actors like me. I hope to give back to the community one day as generously as he did."

Brenda was lost in thought as the conversation moved on around her. She decided she must explore the attic of the bed and breakfast at the first opportunity. She knew much of her uncle's things had been stored in crates there after his death. She had a lot to learn about him. Her thoughts were interrupted when Ellen Teague's voice cut through the chatter.

"I too knew Randolph well," Ellen said, approaching their table. "We were a well-known pair in the early days. We could have enjoyed our fame together if he hadn't decided to suddenly move down to this godforsaken hamlet." She looked around the lawn disparagingly and then turned to Brenda. "We'll have to talk about that later. We must continue with the rehearsal now."

Brenda nodded. She shivered at the tone of voice Ellen had used. The others did not comment on her cold remark and Ellen whisked them back to rehearsal. After the happy spell of the conversation around her had been broken by Ellen, watching the rehearsal seemed to have lost some of its former glamor. She felt the need to be alone. She made sure that her chef Morgan remembered that dinner would be an hour early, to give the cast time to leave for the outdoor theatre at Harbor Park, then climbed the stairs to her rooms.

Once in her apartment, Brenda poured a glass of iced tea and settled back in her easy chair. When this weekend was over, she planned to spend a lot of time in the attic opening crates that held her uncle's past life. It would be an excellent way to relax after Ellen Teague's stressful presence at the bed and breakfast.

That evening, her cell phone rang. Mac told her he would be there in forty-five minutes to pick her up for the performance. The call ended and Brenda quickly showered and got ready. She had read reviews again for the comedy and couldn't wait to see it. She hoped to regain her admiration for Ellen Teague by becoming immersed in the play and forgetting about everything else that had happened. In no time at all, she heard Mac's unmistakable voice filter up the stairs from the front desk. The bed and breakfast had been quiet since the actors had left for Harbor Park. Brenda smiled in anticipation of a wonderful night and picked up the tickets from her bureau and hurried down to meet Mac.

As he took her arm and they walked toward the park, she noticed him glance down at her hand to peek at the delicate promise ring on her finger. "Did you know this play is a comedy of sorts?"

"I know all about it," said Brenda. "I got to see some of the rehearsal. The play takes place at a country estate and then the two main couples switch partners as an experiment. It's sort of like Wife Swap, the reality TV show. I think it's interesting that Ellen gets paired with Shawn. I wonder how she decided that."

"She probably decided since he was so good-looking she had to be paired with him." Mac winked at her. "That's why you agreed to date me, isn't it?"

She jabbed his arm and teased back. As they entered the park, they saw most of the population of Sweetfern Harbor, not to mention a large number of tourists, and they quickly found their seats amid the crowd. One empty seat was next to Brenda and she wondered who would be sitting there. It didn't take long to find out. Edward Graham, her lawyer and a fixture in Sweetfern Harbor, arrived and greeted them warmly.

As they chatted with Edward, Brenda saw that William Pendleton and Phyllis Lindsey were seated only a few rows ahead. Their heads together, they whispered back and forth to one another. Brenda smiled to hear Phyllis's soft laugh. Directly behind them sat Phyllis's daughter Molly, who owned the popular Morning Sun Coffee shop on Main Street, and her boyfriend Pete Graham, the postman who delivered mail around Sweetfern Harbor, including to Sheffield Bed and Breakfast. As they waited for the lights to dim, the conversation between old and new friends was lively. Brenda leaned over to greet Mac's daughter Jenny and her friend Hope, who owned the bakery that supplied pastries to the bed and breakfast. The air of anticipation finally broke when the lights dimmed and all eyes focused on the outdoor stage.

Edward leaned close to Brenda and whispered. "I have some news for you, Brenda. Will you have some time right after the performance to talk?"

She looked at his face. Whatever he had to say must be serious stuff. "I'll see you then," she whispered back. Brenda watched the story unfolding on stage and was soon taken in by Ellen's skills and by the comedic talents of the entire cast. It was easy to forget Ellen's offstage personality as she transformed into a witty and glamorous wife whose ribald lines with Shawn's character had the audience holding their sides with laughter. Anna and Ricky, whose characters had been paired off unhappily in the other wife swap, engineered a hilarious prank in revenge, and the ingénue Bonnie appeared at the end as the young country heiress who saved the day and righted all wrongs. When the lights came down, the audience immediately jumped to their feet in a standing ovation. After three encores and a multitude of bouquets were handed to the actors and actresses, it was agreed by all that "The Rich Game" measured up to everyone's expectations.

"I plan to come back tomorrow if I can get a ticket," said Jenny with enthusiasm. "This is the best show I've seen in a long time."

Everyone around her agreed and immediately began

making plans to come back, but Brenda realized this might be her chance to get to the attic sooner rather than later. She set aside her initial idea to wait until the weekend was over. Seeing such a wonderful play made her determined to delve into her uncle's life right away.

As the crowds thinned, Brenda told Mac to wait a few minutes. "Edward wants to tell me something. I think it must be important since he wanted to talk right after the show."

"Don't worry about me. I'll sit over there on that bench and wait."

Edward suggested they walk a few yards away from everyone. "Ellen Teague met with me earlier today." His eyes avoided hers. "There is a court case involving you and your uncle's estate. She tells me you do not own Sheffield Bed and Breakfast. I don't have all the details yet but it is first on my agenda tomorrow. I won't wait for Monday to find out whether her claims have merit."

Brenda closed her mouth when she realized it was wide open with shock. "But...I was named in his will. He owned the bed and breakfast and he left it to me. That's all there is to it. The will is a legal document. You were his lawyer, Edward, so you should know."

"Simmer down. I told you I still have to get the details, though I doubt she is telling the whole truth of the matter. Still, I will look into it and let you know whatever I find out."

When she returned to Mac she had a heavy heart. Her eyes fell on the cast members who were just then leaving the stage area. A group of fans, journalists, and reporters swarmed toward them, and Ellen Teague stepped forward to claim the center of attention. Even from a distance Brenda could see a few of the actors exchange glances and roll their eyes as Ellen flashed a brilliant smile for the cameras. There was no doubt that Ellen's fame and attitude caused a great deal of tension and Brenda felt sorry for the other actors. They all did a fantastic job on stage. Brenda waited a few moments, watching the hubbub across the park's lawn from where she stood.

Mac didn't ask questions but knew that something was definitely wrong. Whatever it was that Edward Graham had to discuss, it apparently wasn't good news. They watched the actors pose under the starry summer sky for a photo – Ellen posing glamorously in front and the rest of the cast arrayed behind her. When Mac turned to look at Brenda again, for a moment he thought she was about to cry. Then he looked closer and saw that her cheeks were flushed as if with righteous anger.

"Let's go home, Brenda. You look like you need a breather."

Brenda took one more look at the actors, then turned to

nod at Mac. She wanted nothing more than to confront Ellen head-on and find out what this lawsuit was all about.

She allowed Mac to steer her homeward. "I don't want the news getting out but Edward just told me the Sheffield Bed and Breakfast may not belong to me." As Mac turned to look at her in surprise, she told Mac about the blow Edward's news had dealt her.

"He will get to the bottom of this," said Mac. "He filed the will and you signed the papers, I can't imagine what could change that. Let's stop and get a drink to end the night."

They stopped at a small bar and grill at the end of Main Street and sat listening to the live music played by a small acoustic band on the deck that looked out toward the street. She sipped a glass of red wine while he enjoyed a cold beer and they watched the crowds from the theatre festival trickling home down Main Street. It was a beautiful night and she should have been relaxing with the man she loved, but her mind was racing. Brenda finally stifled a yawn and told him she was beat. "I'll talk to you tomorrow. Edward is going to look things over in the morning rather than wait until Monday so I'll call you when I hear something." Mac, still worried about her, walked her home with a protective arm wrapped around her shoulders.

At the door to the bed and breakfast, Mac leaned down.

His kiss lingered longer than usual. She smiled up at him, the warm glow of his embrace permeating her body, and turned to go inside. He waved over his shoulder as he walked back down the street, knowing Brenda would be looking at him from the front windows as she always did. She climbed the stairs wearily to her apartment hoping that Edward would soon have good news for her.

CHAPTER FOUR

SHOCKING NEWS

The Blossoms van pulled up in front of Sheffield Bed and Breakfast the next morning. Allie peeked out the front door and saw Jenny Rivers unloading spray after spray of beautiful bouquets, many of them roses. She went outside to lend a hand.

"Good morning, Jenny. Did Brenda order all these flowers?"

"Not all of them. Most are deliveries for Ellen Teague. There are more of them coming, I'll have to make a second delivery run later today. I'm just hoping I don't run out. If I do, I'll have to get the florist in the next town over to help me out."

Brenda appeared in the doorway just as Allie and Jenny

carried up several armfuls to the front porch. Allie told her most of the flowers were for the famous star.

"I separated yours from Ellen's," said Jenny. She pointed to the cluster set aside on the porch. "As soon as I get them all inside you can tell me where you want them. I have the newspaper with early morning reviews with me, too, if you want an extra copy." Her eyes sparkled. Sweetfern Harbor's visiting star certainly increased business in the village. The whole town had come alive.

"Let's take as many as we can carry up to her room," said Brenda. She solicited Allie's help and the three made their way upstairs.

Brenda knocked on the door. When it opened, she saw Ellen Teague perfectly coiffed and with makeup on, but she was more astonished by the exquisite silk dressing gown she wore. The emerald green silk contrasted with her dark eyes that glittered in the morning sunshine. Brenda did not know if she would get used to this kind of glamor in her bed and breakfast.

Ellen did not appear surprised at the numerous bouquets and immediately directed them where to place each bouquet. The lavish floral displays spilled their incredible perfumes into the room and looked magnificent when set up on the bureau and the dressing table.

"There are more to come," said Jenny. "We'll bring them up right away."

Ellen had no comment and turned back to the mirror where she patted her hair in place. Allie and Jenny started for the door when Ellen decided to speak.

"Bring just a few more up here. The rest can be displayed prominently throughout the bed and breakfast."

Jenny and Allie glanced at Brenda. Her look told them to quickly go and get the rest. As for Brenda, she tried to take a calming breath. Ellen had made a generous offer, but it wasn't the actress's prerogative to command her to place them prominently – but Brenda ignored that for the moment. Brenda took a deep breath and got right to the issue.

"What is this about a court case against my Uncle Randolph's estate challenging me as the rightful owner of the bed and breakfast?"

Ellen turned to look at her briefly, then rolled her eyes dismissively as she stood up to face her. "Oh, you silly girl, you do not own this place. I'm the one with a stronger legal claim to it." She advanced toward Brenda as she said this, and Brenda instinctively took a step back toward the door. "It will all be sorted out soon. This place needs a lot of improvements but I'll manage that. Not that I plan to spend much time here but it is mine nevertheless." Without waiting for a response, she gently pushed Brenda through the doorway with one manicured hand and closed the door in her face.

"You can say what you want, but you can't take the Sheffield Bed and Breakfast from me." Brenda raised her voice slightly to be heard through the closed door, not caring who overheard.

Ellen opened the door a crack, just wide enough to give Brenda another cold look. "You really must get used to the fact that it was never yours in the first place." She closed it again and Brenda heard the lock click.

When she composed herself and returned downstairs, the smell of the armfuls of flowers Allie and Jenny returned with became too much. "I need some fresh air. Jenny, the rest of the flowers should just go to the sitting room for now, I'll deal with them later. Allie, do you want a break?"

"Sure. Is the smell from all these flowers getting to you?"

Brenda thought her beautiful Sheffield house smelled like a funeral home but didn't express those thoughts aloud. "I could use a good walk right now."

They walked down the road toward Main Street. Brenda had never seen so many tourists at one time in Sweetfern Harbor. Not only were tourists visiting for the Seaside Theatre Festival, but reporters and journalists were in town for the duration of the show. Someone pointed out the owner of the Sheffield Bed and Breakfast right as they walked into town and Brenda found herself in the center of a small group of reporters clamoring for details about Ellen Teague.

As she listened to their silly questions, Brenda knew she had had enough of the actress. She finally said, "Please, I cannot divulge anything private about the star, or about any guest of the Sheffield. But I am sure Ellen will give interviews when ready." The disappointed reporters finally left her alone. Brenda and Allie finally reached Morning Sun Coffee in one piece and saw Shawn and Anna Quincy sitting at a table that looked out onto the street. Despite the indignities of hosting Ellen Teague, Brenda was determined that the other actors should have a better experience visiting their tiny town. Allie followed Brenda as she made her way to their table.

"I didn't get a chance to congratulate you both on your stunning performance last night. I thoroughly enjoyed the play and your acting was superb."

"Thank you. We're glad you enjoyed it," said Shawn, flashing her with one of his megawatt smiles. "Ricky has a few comp tickets that Ellen, or rather Chester, gave him if you want to see it again."

Brenda thanked him and told him she was busy, but she was sure Jenny wanted to go again. She didn't say it but privately she wondered if she could possibly enjoy seeing the play again. How could she enjoy seeing her formerly favorite actress on stage, pretending to be this glittering beauty of warmth and charm, when Brenda now knew what she was really like? She knew it wasn't something she was ready for. Shawn agreed he would pass the word on to Ricky to give the extra tickets to Jenny Rivers.

"You're welcome to join us," said Anna, patting the chair next to her and smiling at the still-starstruck Allie.

Brenda left her young employee happily chatting with the Hollywood stars and chatted with Molly, the proprietor, for a few minutes while she ordered their drinks. When their lattés were ready, Brenda carried them from the counter over to the table and sat down to listen as Anna finished telling Allie a hilarious story about a stage makeup mishap that had happened on her very first touring show.

As they finished their lattés, the cheery sound of the bell at the Morning Sun's door rang as more tourists trooped in. Brenda took that as their cue and told Allie they should get back to the bed and breakfast. They said their goodbyes to the Quincys and headed back on Main Street.

More than anything, Brenda reflected, she wanted to be alone. The town, crowded from the festival, began to suffocate her today as it never had before. It was not unlike the feeling she had felt in her bed and breakfast following the uncomfortable confrontation with Ellen. She had a lot to think about.

Upon their return, Brenda spoke to Phyllis and was relieved to hear there wouldn't be a repeat of yesterday's rehearsal on the back lawn. She decided to prepare her own lunch in the main kitchen and take it up the back stairway to her apartment. She needed time to think, but more than anything she hoped Edward Graham would call her soon. Perhaps he found a loophole of some sort or maybe he found out Ellen's claim was not legally sound after all.

Brenda had eaten her lunch and straightened her room when finally her phone rang. She glanced at the screen and saw it was Mac, and answered the call with some relief. He was eager to know if she had heard from Edward yet, and she gave him the disappointing news.

"Well, I'm sure he'll be in touch soon. Meanwhile, I thought I'd go see 'The Rich Game' again tonight. Jenny asked me to take her. She was sure caught up with it and she got complimentary tickets from Ricky Owens." He noted the pause from her end. "I didn't ask you since you gave me the impression you didn't like Ellen Teague so much now."

"It's perfectly fine. Your daughter wants to see it again and I'm not really interested. For the record, I still admire Ellen's talent but not so much her personality offstage. Have a good time tonight." She meant her last words, but she felt strange, almost lonely, knowing he didn't ask her first.

"I'm just being silly," she told herself when they had hung up. "Jenny really wants to see it again and why shouldn't Mac take her?"

In an attempt to distract herself, she thought again about the magnificent stories she had heard about her Uncle Randolph from the actors who had known him. What else did she not know about him? Could Ellen's claim have some merit? It was a troublesome thought.

She knew Randolph had married three times and never had a child of his own. The one time she had visited Sheffield house with her parents, her uncle had taken her up the narrow stairs to what she now knew was the attic. He showed her a playroom with a slanted ceiling and faded old wallpaper in a floral pattern. With a proud flourish, he opened the floor-to-ceiling cupboards to show her the old toys stored there, and then in the final cupboard he showed her a large antique dollhouse with all its furnishings. She had played with the delicate, tiny furniture and porcelain doll figures for hours while the adults talked downstairs. He seemed to find great happiness in her joy that day, like it was a secret he had been longing to share with just the right person. It was an enchanting memory, one she cherished. Not until she was in her teens had her parents mentioned him again, and only to mention how he had transformed the old mansion into a bed and breakfast. It wasn't until decades later that she learned he too never forgot his niece and that captivating visit to the attic playroom. After his death, her uncle's lawyer Edward Graham contacted her to inform her she was the heiress of his estate and now the proud owner of Randolph Sheffield's bed and breakfast.

Quiet descended on the Sheffield house as the day wore on into the late afternoon and still no phone call came from Edward. Brenda waited and finally drifted off to sleep in her chair and awoke with a start. Aside from the ticking of the hall clock, there was not a sound throughout the huge house. She remembered then that the cast and crew of the play had reserved dinner at one of the upscale restaurants at the edge of town with a waterfront view. It was time to discover who her uncle really was.

Brenda climbed the narrow stairs to the attic with a heavy-duty screwdriver in her hand. She switched on the light and walked through the first couple of empty rooms, toward the room farthest from the stairs where she knew her uncle's crates were stored. The revelation that he had once been an actor opened up a whole new chapter in his life as far as she was concerned. Even more fascinating to her was the fact that he had been connected to Ellen Teague, and that these crates could hold the key to that story.

Brenda opened the dusty room and brushed away a cobweb that hung from the light. She looked at the stacks of wooden crates and old-fashioned steam trunks before her. She lifted a crate down from one pile and read the handwritten note on the outside, "Costumes." Setting it down for later, she looked at the second crate which read, more promisingly, "Memorabilia." She pried open the top of the crate with her screwdriver, the nails squeaking in the wood, until she could take the lid off. Inside she found a treasure trove of Broadway tickets, advertising posters, and playbills. Randolph Sheffield's name was on everything. Brenda sat back on her heels in satisfaction.

"You really were an actor, Uncle Randolph. Why did I never know that?"

As hard as she tried, Brenda could not remember either parent talking about his days as an actor. As she sifted through several other boxes of memorabilia and other papers, Brenda found a small bundle of letters tied with a heavy string. The one on top was addressed to her father. It was stamped but had not been mailed. She turned it over and saw that it had not been sealed either. Perhaps Randolph had more to say and had never finished writing it. She unfolded the two sheets of paper and began reading.

In the letter, Randolph explained his frustrations to his brother, her father, Tim. Evidently this had been written during the run of a play in which he and Ellen Teague had been costars. Randolph wrote that he was tired of playing second fiddle to Ellen Teague. She hogged the spotlight until reporters started zeroing in on her alone.

She played one character for the public, another character on the stage, and a nasty character in private, even in those days. She had played the press like a fiddle – so well, in fact, that her costar Randolph had barely merited a mention in the reviews that praised her talents and beauty. It had been a bitter pill to swallow for her uncle.

Brenda clutched the letter tighter, feeling a kinship through the years with her uncle. As she read on, she softened as she read that Randolph was in love with someone named Anne. No last name was provided in the letter. Ellen had snubbed him until she found out about Anne, and then Ellen found a million ways to sabotage him. She found ways to interrupt them, or show up when he was out on a date. She was not afraid to use her star power to try to ruin Randolph's chance at happiness.

In the last paragraph, Randolph told his brother he wanted out of show business. He missed the pleasures of living in a small town like the one the two brothers grew up in, in upstate New York. The next sentence began: *I have a chance to buy a historic home in a town called Sweetfern Harbor. I've visited there several times and have decided to purchase it. It is right on the...* here the words ended. This confirmed what Brenda thought: that her uncle had more to say or he would have mailed the letter to her father. She wondered what interrupted him and why he didn't go back and finish the letter. There was no way to answer that. The two brothers, along with her mother, were now deceased.

It dawned on her that she and her uncle were very much alike. He wanted a simpler life and so did she. When she had found out the bed and breakfast was hers, she discovered how much the town of Sweetfern Harbor and its life of simplicity and freedom drew her in. The townspeople had accepted her and it didn't take long for her to feel right at home for the first time in her life. She put her life as assistant to a Private Investigator back in Michigan aside. She had enjoyed her role as an amateur sleuth but was ready for peace and quiet in a quaint village set along the Atlantic Ocean. That didn't mean she would stop reading crime novels, though.

Whatever happened between Ellen Teague and Randolph Sheffield fed her curiosity. On the other hand, as hostess to the famous actress, she knew her first priority was to apologize to her guest for her behavior that morning and make things right again. She would have to set aside the terrible business of the court case and treat Ellen Teague just like any other guest.

Brenda closed up the attic again and returned to her room. She stretched out across her bed and flipped through an old script that she had come across in the crates. Immersed in the old-fashioned murder mystery play, she did not realize it was getting late until a cold breeze sailed through her curtains and made her shiver.

She absently stayed awake reading until she heard everyone come in. She listened as doors closed and everyone started settling in for the night. Then she went down to Ellen's room and knocked on her door. Chester opened the door with expectant, raised eyebrows.

Brenda opened her mouth to speak but stopped when she heard another familiar voice. She looked past Chester and saw William Pendleton sitting in one of the wingback armchairs with a glass of champagne in his hand. Chester stepped aside as William turned to greet her, but Brenda chose to focus on Ellen.

"I'm sorry to interrupt, I just wanted to speak with Miss Teague. I can do that in the morning..."

"No, don't let me trouble you. I must be on my way," said William. Chester excused himself as well, saying he needed to see to the costumes that had been brought to his room.

Ellen looked down her nose at the interruption. "The costumes will have to be dry-cleaned again by tomorrow afternoon. It's our last performance here and I want them to look perfect."

"I'll let Allie know," said Brenda, as she watched William and Chester leave. She felt unaccountably nervous when she was left alone with Ellen. "I came to apologize for my bad behavior earlier. I hope you have found everything satisfactory during your stay here."

"I don't really care about your apology or anyone else's for that matter. If that is all, then I'll say goodnight—"

"That's not all. I was reading through my uncle's papers today. I only just found out that Randolph was an actor, and that you knew him, but I'm not sure how important you were to him at the time." Brenda knew she was only stirring up something she had come in to defuse but felt helpless to stop herself.

Ellen turned to regard Brenda silently for a moment before she said, "Randolph and I had a very…close relationship in those days. When he told me he was moving to Sweetfern Harbor I told him it was a huge mistake on his part. He was an actor with real talent but he threw it all away." For a moment, Brenda saw bitterness behind the actress's cool demeanor. "He always said he would turn this place into a bed and breakfast. I see that he reached his goal, though for the life of me I don't know why he would want to demean himself and his talents this way."

Ellen paused as if waiting for a certain reaction. Brenda was determined not to give her the satisfaction of rising to the bait of such a hateful comment.

Instead, Brenda bit back her harsher words and replied evenly, "This is an honorable business – and a successful one I might add – and he recognized it as such. My uncle did much good around this community and was known as a mentor and benefactor."

Ellen waved her hand in dismissal of Brenda's words. "Never mind all of that. The people in a town like this couldn't possibly understand who he was truly meant to be. I spoke to Edward Graham again today. Once the Seaside Theatre Festival is finished and I'm back in New York I plan to file suit against the Sheffield estate for ownership of this establishment." Her chuckle bordered on a sneer. "Randolph promised me this house. And I don't plan to keep it in this sorry state, either. I plan to rehab the whole place and turn it back into a luxury estate for myself."

"Are you telling me that if you win this lawsuit, and you won't, that you will live here in Sweetfern Harbor?" Brenda could hardly believe her ears.

"Are you crazy? I don't plan on living here, but it will make a nice vacation home – perhaps one or two weeks in the summer. Who knows, I may discover what drove Randolph to choose this backwater town over me."

Brenda shook her head and fought to keep her anger at bay. She felt it seeping upward again, coloring her cheeks, and was powerless to hold her tongue. "You don't deserve this...this backwater. And you will never get this bed and breakfast, so don't count on it!"

She turned and swept out the door, slamming it behind her. It wasn't until she stood in the hall, fuming, that she realized the volume of her voice must have reached through the walls. She heard another soft chuckle through Ellen's closed door and the click of the lock.

Brenda's eyes swam with tears of frustration as she returned to her apartment. But she refused to let those tears fall where anyone might see. The stress of the last few days overtook Brenda and as soon as she climbed into her own bed, her tears rolled down her cheeks until she finally turned over and sank into a fitful sleep.

CHAPTER FIVE

THE BODY

The next morning at breakfast, Brenda sat with Phyllis, who noticed her boss was quieter than usual.

"What's the matter, Brenda?"

Brenda shook her head. "It's something I have to figure out by myself and I plan to get right on it as soon as our guests leave for their final performance."

Phyllis gently prodded again but to no avail. She finally patted Brenda's arm and told her when she was ready to talk about it she would be there for her. The two women sat in the quiet of the morning, gazing at the crystal-clear view of the Atlantic Ocean from the window of the sitting room as they enjoyed their coffee. Neither had a hint of what was to come only moments later when Shawn Quincy burst into the room with his fatal news.

"She's dead."

———

After Brenda had entered the room and found Ellen Teague motionless atop her bed, she ushered the curious actors away, instructed Chester to let no one near the room, and quickly returned to the first floor. As she called 911 from the front desk and told the dispatcher to send an ambulance, she looked across the hall into the sitting room only to see Shawn Quincy sitting in an armchair as Phyllis patted his shoulder soothingly. The actor was expressionless and Brenda supposed he must have been in mild shock.

In a short time, she heard the wail of sirens as they approached the bed and breakfast. Mac Rivers was the first one through the door, and he gave Brenda a quick, worried look as she led him and the paramedic crew up to Ellen's door. The other actors stood in a group a few feet away in the hallway. Allie and Phyllis remained rooted at the top of the stairs. No one spoke a word. The ambulance crew rushed in behind the detective and Brenda. She watched as the two paramedics quickly checked the actress for vital signs. She had no pulse, no breath, and the body was already cold, so resuscitation would have no effect. The lead paramedic shook her head ruefully.

"I'm calling it in," she said. She examined the inert body on the bed again. "I'll get the coroner here." She turned away to make a phone call.

Brenda watched Mac closely and saw him looking at Ellen's body and her surroundings with the practiced eye of a detective. She looked around too and several details were immediately apparent. Empty champagne glasses were scattered on the two small bedside tables. It looked as if Ellen finished off the bottle after everyone left her room the night before. There was a belt Brenda recognized from the green satin dressing gown she wore the evening before when they had their unpleasant encounter. The belt dangled loosely from the corner post of the bed. Red marks stood out lividly on the ashen flesh of Ellen's throat.

"Looks like strangulation," said Mac. "I'd say that belt could be the weapon. Doesn't look like hands did it, but of course that's up to the coroner to decide."

Brenda nodded in agreement with Mac's assessment. The overwhelming odor of the bouquets and vases of flowers caused a sickened lurch in the pit of Brenda's stomach. The windows were shut tight and the air in the room was uncomfortably warm. Brenda itched to open a window but knew she couldn't touch anything.

Mac continued to walk around the room. He pulled on gloves and fingered a card in a plastic holder sticking out of an especially large vase of red roses. Brenda stepped closer to examine it alongside him.

"Read this," he said. Brenda saw the words 'Good Riddance' on the card. There was no signature.

Mac motioned for another officer who had arrived with him and asked him to put the note in a bag and to gather any other evidence he could find. "Take that vase of roses, too. And the shiny green belt, of course."

They heard the coroner arrive – in the strange quiet that had descended on the bed and breakfast, Brenda could discern each voice downstairs as Allie ushered him in. The coroner arrived with a photographer assistant who took a number of photographs during the coroner's examination. It didn't take long for him to pronounce her dead and to fill out the appropriate paperwork. Not much longer after that, the paramedics brought their gurney to the room and took out an extra sheet to wrap the body for privacy from the prying eyes of the public who had gathered on the sidewalk outside. Brenda watched, half in shock, as Ellen's body was wheeled out to the ambulance for transportation to the morgue.

Mac touched Brenda's arm gently and searched her eyes for reassurance.

"Brenda, I need your help. No one is allowed to leave the

premises until we have interviewed them all." Brenda nodded, firmly pushing away the shocking events and vowing to focus on supporting Mac. "Are there other guests here besides the actors?"

Brenda told him of the two regulars. The couple had peeked into the hall during the commotion and their faces had paled when Ellen's body was taken away. The woman had turned and Brenda had distinctly heard her lose her breakfast. The husband hurriedly closed the door and they had not emerged since.

"The officer will be dusting for fingerprints and gathering as much evidence as possible. It won't be the last search in here, so please inform your staff and the other guests that the room is strictly off limits." Brenda nodded. He walked toward Chester who had not moved from his post in the doorway of his room since the body had been wheeled out of the room. His face was hard to read, but, Brenda reflected, that was no different than it had been since his arrival. "Mr. Boyd, I will begin with you. Let's go to your room where we can talk in private."

Chester stepped into his room and Mac followed him as an officer strung yellow crime scene tape across the hallway door to Ellen's room. Mac was surprised to see that Chester's room had an interior door with direct access to Ellen's room. He was satisfied he chose the assistant as his first interviewee. He offered his condolences to Chester and opened with a few easy questions about their stay at Sheffield Bed and Breakfast so far, and the star's daily routines. Then he got right to the point.

"When did you last see Ellen Teague?"

"I last saw her alive late last night, around eleven o'clock. She had a guest in her room and the three of us drank champagne to celebrate the success of the play. The guest left when Miss Sheffield came to speak with Miss Teague. I left for my room before they spoke. Before I could get into bed I had to get the costumes bundled up for dry-cleaning. Miss Sheffield had arranged for that per Miss Teague's orders."

The detective noted that Chester's face hardly betrayed any emotion. He reflected that perhaps the actress's assistant was in shock, as often happened to close associates of a murder victim. Mac asked if he knew why the owner of the bed and breakfast came to Ellen's room so late at night.

"I presume to check if there was anything else Miss Teague needed. We had just returned after the performance. Miss Sheffield has been very good about making sure we are all taken care of." When asked, Chester told Mac the guest who visited was William Pendleton. "He came in to visit and congratulate her on the performance. They had met before and so were acquainted."

"That's all my questions for now. I am very sorry for your loss, but no one is allowed to leave the premises," said Mac. "I will want to question you again, I'm sure."

"We'll all be right here. There is one final performance before we leave town."

"So the play won't be canceled in light of her death?" Mac was surprised to hear this.

"Oh, no, the show will go on. That's how it always is."

"Who will play Miss Teague's part?" asked Mac.

"I suppose it will be Bonnie or possibly Anna. Ricky will figure out how to make it all work." Chester sat on his bed with his hands calmly folded as Mac thanked him and walked out of the room.

Mac walked away shaking his head. He had enjoyed the play but was shocked that the show would go on even after the star's death. But seeing Chester's calm demeanor, he didn't doubt it would. Mac looked for Brenda again and gave her a nod. She stood talking to Phyllis and Allie, but turned to address the actors who stood milling around the second-floor hallway.

"Everyone please go downstairs for a late breakfast. I know this has been a difficult morning, but Detective Rivers will want to speak to each one of you. Please don't leave the premises until he says it's all right to do so."

The cast was subdued and in shock. Brenda studied each

face as they passed her. Nothing gave her any ideas of who did this. When she reflected on the strained relationship between Ellen and the other cast members, there was no doubt in her mind that any of them would be relieved to have her gone – but dead? It seemed unthinkable. But the killer was clearly among them. She turned when Mac called to her.

"Who found the body?"

She walked over to where he stood looking through his notes. "Shawn Quincy. He told Phyllis that he went into her room to fetch a script. The door was unlocked and she didn't answer, so he assumed she was already down at breakfast. But Mac, wouldn't Chester have heard him knocking?"

"Chester told me he always waited for her to call for him in the mornings. When she was ready for him, she would call for him to enter, but he was never to go in until then."

Brenda paused, thinking. "Did the coroner determine time of death?"

"That's the puzzling part. He said he couldn't give a precise time until after his full examination, but based on the temperature of her body she had been dead for quite a few hours. What happened when you spoke to her last night?"

"I tried to apologize about something I said, but it didn't go over too well. I was angry and slammed the door on the way out. She locked it. I heard the latch turn."

Mac stopped and stared at her. "You and Ellen Teague argued last night? What was that all about?"

Brenda held her breath for a moment as she realized this must sound suspicious. "I came to her room after everyone got back, to apologize for an earlier argument I had with her. You have to understand, she said terrible things about my uncle and she still claims the bed and breakfast was meant for her. I lost my temper the first time and came to apologize for my bad behavior, hoping to put it behind us. Instead, she just insisted she would file suit against the estate to get Sheffield Bed and Breakfast." Brenda looked down, afraid to meet his eyes. "I'm afraid I shouted at her and told her she would never get it. I'm sorry. It was the wrong thing to do."

Mac decided to store this information in the back of his head for now, but it troubled him. "What's more important is that we need to find out who unlocked Ellen Teague's door. If we can answer this question, we'll be well on our way." Brenda nodded in relief and agreement and followed him down the stairs. When the detective and owner walked into the dining room, the cast were discussing details of the last performance of "The Rich Game."

"I know every line," Chester was saying. "I can be the country estate host, instead of a hostess, freeing up

Bonnie to take over Ellen's part." Ricky chimed in that he agreed it was the most logical solution. Brenda noticed a curious lack of tears among the actors, though Bonnie sat quietly stirring her mug of tea and not joining in the conversation, despite the favorable new casting decision.

Mac singled out Shawn Quincy and led him away from the table and asked Brenda to join them. They went into the sitting room where they closed the doors in order to speak privately.

"Do you have any idea who may have unlocked Miss Teague's room sometime early this morning or perhaps last night?"

"I have no idea," said Shawn. "Every cast member has a key to the room." Brenda's head jerked up at this detail, which was news to her. "Ellen told Chester to have keys made for all of us so we would have access in case she was out. If the room was unlocked, we knew that meant someone else had already been in there and it was all right for the rest of us to do the same. I don't know who went in first."

Inwardly, Brenda seethed thinking of the lack of concern for safety Ellen Teague had displayed by her actions, to say nothing of her audacity to copy keys without permission. She made a mental note to have the lock changed on that door once the investigation was completed.

After questioning, Shawn stated he had been in his room with his wife all night once they were back at the bed and breakfast.

"Did either of you leave the room at all once you arrived back here?"

"Anna left for maybe twenty minutes to use the Wi-Fi in the lobby. She had to email her agent in New York City," he said. "She mentioned talking briefly with Allie. I'm sure she will vouch for Anna. I watched TV for a while until she got back. That was around ten o'clock. I remember the time since neither of us was interested in watching the news. We were bushed and decided to get a good night's sleep."

"Is there anyone who can vouch for you that you didn't leave the room while your wife was downstairs?"

The actor looked taken aback momentarily. "Well, no, I was alone until she returned. As I said, I watched TV until she came back." He glanced at Brenda. "Both of us woke up when we heard you and Ellen. We laughed since it was rare that anyone stood up to her like that." He quickly amended his words. "We didn't know what was said but it sounded as if you were winning."

Brenda felt a flush rise to her face. "I apologize for my behavior, and for awakening you."

Shawn smiled, evidently still savoring the experience of overhearing Ellen's comeuppance, and waved her apology aside. Mac looked at Brenda's flushed cheeks. It was unnerving to hear about the argument again. Mac shook his head at the impossible thoughts that came to him. He excused Shawn from the interview and thanked him for his time.

"I guess his words will have to be taken as truth for now," said Brenda. "There is no one except his wife to say he stayed there all night long. That's a question to ask the others. Maybe someone saw if anybody left their rooms in the middle of the night."

"That's true. We have to take his word for now. And of course we'll have the fingerprints from Ellen's room."

"Yes, but I'm sure he will find mine and the fingerprints of the staff who clean in there. And there will be every cast member's prints, including Chester's. Not only were members of the show coming and going for costumes but their scripts and some of the smaller props were in there as well."

Mac took a breath and held it before letting it escape. "You are right about that. Everyone who has been in that room is a suspect." He called to Allie who was leaving the desk. She confirmed the alibi Shawn gave for his wife.

"If Shawn heard you when his wife got back upstairs then he couldn't have done it while she was gone. She obviously was still alive at that point." Mac paced a few steps, still bothered by his nagging thoughts. He turned to look at Brenda with tension furrowing his brow. "How angry were the two of you to be yelling like that?"

"I told you exactly what happened," Brenda said. She felt herself shut down. She realized that Mac looked at her as a possible suspect. After all they had gone through, he did not trust her word. The blow she felt in that moment was as if he had physically knocked her to the floor.

Sooner or later, he would question her. She did not know if she could bear to hear those doubts spoken out loud. She closed her eyes for a brief moment and touched the promise ring on her finger.

Mac was still intent on his thought process and continued to pace. "Did William Pendleton visit Ellen more than the one time you observed him?"

Brenda forced herself to answer normally, though she could feel herself wanting to run away or panic. "I don't know if he did or not. He could have. This is a big place and I'm not always at the entrance or on this floor for that matter. My guests relax and interact as they wish."

"I will interview him next. He may have a clue I can go on. Maybe he saw someone heading upstairs when he left."

"He was in her room when I came in. He should be interviewed as you are doing everyone else."

Mac noted her set jawline. She was savvy enough to

know he had to consider her as a suspect along with everyone else. "I will talk with William Pendleton. I have my doubts he was involved in a murder...but I'll have to get to him after I deal with your guests."

Brenda knew Mac admired William. After the death of William's wife, he had been very benevolent toward the people of Sweetfern Harbor. Mac Rivers was devoted to his town and often commented on how peaceful things had become after William had gained control of the wealth of properties that had been controlled by his greedy, unhappy wife before her death.

Brenda turned away and mumbled she would see Mac later. She felt sure if she stayed another moment, he would probably just ask her to leave in case she influenced the investigation. And it was agony to see the man she loved extend the benefit of doubt to William Pendleton but not to her own circumstances. But she resolutely refused to dwell on this. She went to the office to check with Allie on who the next guests would be when the cast of "The Rich Game" left. If the play would go on as normal, then so would the Sheffield Bed and Breakfast.

CHAPTER SIX

MORE QUESTIONS

*M*ac Rivers asked Phyllis for a cup of coffee and wearily flipped through his notes. It had been a long morning already and it was still not over. Luckily, William Pendleton had shown up at the bed and breakfast without even being called. He had come to support Phyllis, and had easily agreed to wait with the actors for his own turn to be interviewed. Mac signaled William from the small group waiting in the dining room. He realized he still expected to see Brenda behind him but she was nowhere in sight. He sat across from William in the sitting room and asked him to recount his movements of the night before until this morning.

"Phyllis and I walked back here after the performance ended. It was a beautiful night. We both like to walk on these lovely summer nights. We went directly to her apartment in the back of the bed and breakfast." William smiled fondly. "I've tried to get her to move in with me – that rambling house I live in is too big for just one person and needs a woman's touch – but she likes her independence. It may take time, but I'll convince her soon to marry me." He appeared to drift off in his thoughts until Mac drew him back in with another question.

"How long were you with Phyllis?"

"Perhaps twenty minutes? She brought out cups of tea and cookies and we enjoyed that until we heard the actors come in at the front door. Her oatmeal raisin cookies are hard to resist but I wanted to congratulate the cast before everyone headed to bed. Phyllis said she was tired and had seen them every day since their arrival anyway. To be honest, Mac, I was glad she stayed behind. I was drawn to Ellen in a lot of ways. She was a great actress and not bad to look at."

Mac's eyes cast a look of frank disbelief at the older gentleman.

"Oh no, it was nothing like that," William added hastily. "Phyllis is my true love. But I admire Ellen, and we had met on several occasions. We conversed easily together unlike many who found her too aloof. She called Chester in to open champagne. She was in quite a celebratory mood. The three of us sat down and were drinking it when Brenda came to the door. Any alcohol makes me sleepy right away. I used to be able to handle it better. When Brenda came to the door it gave me an excuse to leave before I fell asleep right there. I didn't see Phyllis again since she told me she was going to bed after I left for Ellen's room."

"Did you see anyone in the hallways when you left?"

He shook his head no. "Everyone must have been in their rooms, I assumed. By then, it was close to eleven or after."

"Did you see anyone around the office or front entrance on your way out?"

Again, his answer was in the negative. Mac excused him to go home if he wanted and next he asked Ricky Owens to join him in the sitting room. The actor's light brown hair matched his neatly trimmed beard. Mac assessed his age to be near his own early forties. He was aware that this actor was well-known in the theatre world. The detective had done his homework and found that Ricky Owens had won many acting awards. He had also been acclaimed since being cast in several roles opposite Ellen Teague. He reached for Mac's hand and the firm handshake was sure. Mac gestured for him to sit down and was impressed that Ricky, like the other actors, appeared well in control of his emotions despite the events of that morning. But he immediately wished to have a second set of eyes to confirm his impressions of the actor.

"If you don't mind, I'd like to have Brenda in here on these interviews. Excuse me for a moment and I'll find her." Mac walked out into the hall, thinking back to the look on Brenda's face before she had left the room earlier.

Brenda walked out of the office just as Mac came out of the sitting room. He asked her to join him again. "I thought you were going to stay with me during these interviews. I need your input." His eyes teased a little. "You are good at this, Brenda. You know I've always admired you for your investigative work back in Michigan."

This gave Brenda the boost to her ego she needed after the incident earlier between them, so she swallowed her fears and rejoined him. They all three settled comfortably in the paisley chairs. Brenda was happy that Mac trusted her enough to keep her around for the interviews, after all. Perhaps she had overreacted to his earlier remarks.

"I want to hear what you did after you arrived back here last night, Mr. Owens," said Mac.

"It had been a long night. Our fans swarmed around wanting autographs after the show. Ellen of course liked to keep the crowds there for as long as possible." Ricky laughed softly. "The truth was that Ellen loved to bask in her glory. She had the habit of pushing the rest of us aside when someone asked for an autograph. She would then scribble her name on whatever the fan pushed toward her. Ellen was like that. She always had to be in the limelight." He grinned. "It's just the way she is – was. It was irritating to all of us at times, but what could we do?"

Brenda bit her lip. With Ricky's joking attitude it was hard to tell if Ellen's "irritating" habits were really the full story. "When you got home, what did you do next?" she asked.

"I went straight to bed. We had one last performance coming up and I was too exhausted to celebrate with anyone. Besides, we usually have a bigger celebration in New York after the last show. But I guess Ellen was celebrating. I saw the champagne glasses."

Brenda and Mac stared at him. "Have you been in her room since her death?" Mac asked.

"I haven't been in there at all. I knew my costume wouldn't be ready until early afternoon. I saw the champagne remnants from the open doorway while we all waited out in the hall. It was while the coroner was in her room."

"Can you say for sure you did not leave your room once you settled in last night?" asked Mac.

"There is no one to vouch for me, but I can say for sure I did not leave my room once I arrived back here. I admit I was still awake when I heard loud voices coming from her room." He didn't mention Brenda's voice in particular, for which she was grateful.

When Ricky Owens left the sitting room, Mac and Brenda discussed the fact that there was no real way to prove whether Ricky Owens was in bed all night long, and alone, or not. He seemed to be upfront and honest. He certainly didn't hold back on how the others felt about Ellen Teague's ego and leadership style. But despite his smooth and polite exterior, Brenda couldn't help but think that Ricky was holding something back.

Bonnie Ross was next in line for an interview. Brenda had been paying close attention to everyone's hands. Ricky's had been sinewy and strong looking. Shawn Quincy's hands were slender and more refined from years of training as a dancer. She looked at Bonnie's hands as the young woman settled herself into the chair in front of her. Overall, she was a bit overweight but curvy and with delicate features. Her hands with their delicate pink manicured nails didn't look strong enough to wield a belt around someone's neck enough to strangle them. Brenda realized that the murderer would have to be strong enough to manage it without letting Ellen making a sound to alert her assistant through the adjoining door.

Why hadn't Chester heard anything? Brenda recalled how often she had witnessed him responding to Ellen when she called for him, no matter how far away from her he was.

"I was in bed asleep the whole night," said Bonnie as Mac

began the questioning. "I was so excited, but a girl needs her beauty sleep. This is my first play and to be working with Ellen Teague is icing on the cake." She laughed and then blushed. "That is – it was. I can't believe she's gone."

"How did you personally feel about Ellen?" Bonnie drew back a little at the penetrating gaze the detective gave her.

"I reveled in the chance to act on stage right next to someone as talented and well-known as Ellen. I know the other actors complained about her, called her narcissistic. I don't deny that she wasn't always easy to work with but I tried not to let it bother me."

"Did you hear anything unusual in the middle of the night?" Mac asked.

Bonnie shot a wide-eyed glance toward Brenda and hesitated.

"Go ahead and tell us everything," Brenda said, knowing what caused her hesitation.

"Well, I heard arguing in the hall. I think I had been asleep maybe an hour or so. It was your voice, Brenda, right? I heard you and Ellen arguing. That's what woke me up, but once things settled down again I was back into a deep sleep."

Brenda expressed an apology to her guest for the disturbance. Bonnie waved it off. "You weren't the first person to argue with Ellen," she said with a dimpled smile, "but I have to admit I believe you were the first to get the last word in."

After Bonnie was excused, Mac looked at Brenda with an unreadable expression. "It seems your argument with Ellen Teague left quite an impression." Brenda was once more chagrined and looked away from the man she loved, trying to gather her thoughts.

"Mac, no one here doubts my commitment to the Sheffield Bed and Breakfast..." she paused and swallowed nervously, trying to gain courage. "I'm happy to answer any questions you have for me, at any time." He nodded and thanked her for being so open, but privately he still wondered.

Mac shuffled his notes and left the room to fetch Anna Quincy. She was the only guest remaining to be interviewed before they would proceed to speak with Brenda's staff members Phyllis Lindsey and Allie Williams. Mac knew he also needed to interview Chester Boyd again. He had no reason to suspect him in particular, but the assistant knew the star better than anyone else, to say nothing of his easy access to her room.

"Did you like Ellen Teague?" Mac directed his first question to Anna when she was settled in the sitting room with him and Brenda.

"I admired her and was grateful she cast me in the plays

she helped produce and direct and star in, but as for liking her, Ellen was not an easy person to like."

"I would think if she continued to give you important parts that you could overlook her shortcomings." Brenda kept her eyes on Anna for a reaction, but the young actress held her gaze with seeming honesty and openness.

"To be honest with you, I had an argument with her only an hour before the performance yesterday. She knew I was good in this role, it was a bigger and better part than I'd had the chance to act in before. But she told me that in the next play I would have a very minor role. I was very unhappy to hear that from her and we argued back and forth a little bit... I felt almost as if she tried to start a fight with me just before the performance to throw me off my game." Brenda couldn't help but wonder if anyone else had witnessed that particular argument.

When questioned further, Anna explained that Ellen was fond of typecasting her as the dumb blonde in the stage comedies she liked to produce back in New York. "I only took those parts to get ahead, not to make a career out of them. Shawn told me Ellen knew I was good and didn't want me to outshine her."

Brenda found that assessment eerily similar to the behavior her Uncle Randolph had described from many years ago. It seemed that sabotage was Ellen's specialty, and she had only gotten better at it as her fame and career had advanced. After Mac dismissed Anna, he turned to Brenda. "What do you think?"

"I think she had motive. Maybe she and Shawn did it together. I've seen how protective he is of Anna." Brenda reminded Mac of the incident they had witnessed in Harbor Park after the performance on opening night. "The press and all those fans were heading toward Shawn and Anna too until Ellen walked out. She stole the spotlight from the other actors in there. It appears none of them liked her but held on to move careers ahead." She stood up to go. "I think that's the last of them. You did interview the couple staying in the far wing, didn't you?"

"I ruled them out. We'll fingerprint them too, but I'm sure they had nothing to do with it. They are shaken up over the whole incident." Mac tapped his pen on his notepad absently and she suddenly knew what he was waiting to ask. "I need to ask you questions now, too, Brenda. You knew this was coming." Brenda nodded and sat back down. "Your relationship was certainly strained once you found out that Ellen meant to take the Sheffield Bed and Breakfast away from you."

Brenda stared at him. "I told you everything I know about that – Edward never called me so I don't know if he found out anything more. I told you about the argument that everyone seems to have heard. It was bad timing, but it was just an argument. And I don't deny it. But I didn't step foot in that room until Shawn came to tell me she was dead. Are you calling me a suspect?"

"Everyone is a suspect, Brenda. And especially anyone who had a motive and you did have motive." Mac told her he was on his way to see Edward Graham. "I have to find out more details about the case against you and the Sheffield estate."

He didn't deny she was a suspect. She could feel her heart pounding in her chest painfully.

"You really don't know me at all, do you Mac Rivers?" Brenda rolled the promise ring around on her finger. "If you did, you would be looking for the real killer."

"I have to look at everyone." He stood and left without saying goodbye, aware of the awkwardness of the situation.

After he left to go to the lawyer's office, she took the ring off and slipped it into her pocket.

Mac drove his squad car to Edward Graham's office as fast as he could safely allow himself to go, but his mind was racing even faster. The more Mac thought about the events between Brenda and Ellen, the more he seethed. How could he be questioning someone he was sure he was in love with? Had he been falling for a woman capable of murder? He parked and hurried into the lawyer's office. Tracy, Edward's paralegal, told him Mr. Graham was working at his desk. When she buzzed his office, he told her to send Mac in.

"Edward, I need to know the details of the lawsuit against Brenda and the Sheffield estate. It may have bearing on a murder investigation." Mac's jaw tensed as Edward turned to regard him seriously.

"It's true that Ellen Teague was bent on suing for ownership of the Sheffield Bed and Breakfast. In fact, Ellen had an appointment with me today to deliver the final version of the lawsuit against the Sheffield estate, she had her lawyer in New York draw it up before she came to town, evidently. She had already brought me a draft of it...she told me she wanted to get it moving along before she left for New York City after the last performance."

"I need details of that lawsuit."

Edward opened his computer and then printed a hard copy. He handed it to the detective. "Ellen was adamant that Randolph promised her the establishment. In the lawsuit, she states that she was to retrieve proof of his promise and provide it in court. She swore she had proof of his intentions."

"But I thought his will named Brenda as his sole heir."

"You're correct. I took care of that for Randolph and

notified Brenda as soon as the will was to be read. The question is, what date is on the so-called proof Ellen Teague had? If it was after the will, then Ellen's claim perhaps would have been a strong one." Edward tilted his chair back and clasped his hands behind his head. "Ellen was determined to fight her case in court."

"She didn't appear to be someone who would enjoy running a bed and breakfast."

Edward laughed ruefully. "She didn't plan to keep it as a business. In fact, I don't believe she was as interested in owning the place as much as she was in winning it from Brenda. Ours was not a pleasant meeting. She hinted that she and Randolph didn't part on good terms once he decided to leave show business."

"Then why would he give it to her?"

"According to Ellen, it was a token of their former relationship. A promise made because he naively hoped she would join him in his love of Sweetfern Harbor. But Randolph must have forgotten all about it, if what she says is true. This is all an act of revenge of some sort on her part."

Detective Rivers felt torn, learning all this from Edward. He hated to think of Brenda losing the Sheffield Bed and Breakfast, but he had to admit that it seemed like a very strong motivation. As he returned to his car, he knew he needed to talk with Brenda again. The more he thought about her, the more he wondered if she had made one very bad decision following that argument, and was now using her connection to him to cover her tracks. Her motives were stronger than anyone interviewed so far. Furthermore, she had the strength to do it. He had seen her lift furniture and other heavy objects when rearranging rooms in the bed and breakfast. He had visited one day to help with a small renovation project and had been surprised to see Brenda was so strong. She handled heavy armchairs as if they were light as a feather.

CHAPTER SEVEN

PRIME SUSPECT

Mac drove to the bed and breakfast and asked Allie to get Brenda. When she came from the kitchen area, he suggested they sit out in the rose garden to continue their talk. Brenda didn't miss his serious expression and thought she denoted a note of sadness in his eyes when he looked at her. She fingered the ring in her pocket as she followed him to the garden and they sat down at a bench under the rose arbor.

"I've talked with Edward Graham. He gave me details of the lawsuit Ellen's lawyer prepared. I read part of it. Her lawyer stated that she has proof that Randolph promised her the property and she would provide that proof in court."

Brenda raised her eyes to meet Mac's with dread. "Was it dated before or after the date on the will?"

"Edward never got to see the proof. Ellen was to send a copy of it as soon as she got back."

"How do we know my uncle actually gave it to her? It doesn't make sense. I didn't tell you this before, but I found one of my uncle's letters in the attic, he told my father he wanted out of show business because of Ellen Teague and the way she treated him. He resented her because she hogged the spotlight and sabotaged him, and he didn't get recognized for his talent even when he was a costar alongside her."

"When did you find that letter?"

"I searched through his crates of belongings in the attic the other night when you took your daughter to the second performance of the play. It was after I found out from the actors that Randolph had been an actor and director. I was clueless that he had a theatre career and I wanted to find out more about him. That's when I found the letter. It was unfinished. He wrote it to my father but never mailed it. In it, he said he couldn't take Ellen Teague any longer. I don't know exactly what that was about, but those were his words. Honestly, I think I know exactly how he felt, too..." Brenda turned to look at Mac as she trailed off, and was horrified to see the cloud of suspicion on his face grow darker.

"Brenda, you continue to prove to me your motives are strongest for wanting her dead. You were upset with her treatment of your uncle and at the same time you had everything to lose. Isn't it true that once Ellen Teague was dead, you had no worries? You get to keep the bed and breakfast and you don't have to face a fight in court. You are an amateur sleuth, and a very good one I might add. Just the kind of person who might know how to hide her tracks. And you are dating the head detective." He finished bitterly, not looking at her.

Brenda jumped to her feet and glared at Mac. She stuffed her hand into her pocket for the ring and it sprang out, falling to the ground. The promise ring bounced on the brick walkway and made a sound like a sad little bell. She retrieved it and pressed it into his hand.

"I don't know what this so-called promise ring meant to you, Mac Rivers, but obviously it meant nothing. If you truly loved me you would know I am not capable of murder. I'm a fighter and I would have gone to court over this and fought with everything I had to defend my uncle's legacy. But I would never, ever commit murder. Not even to get what rightfully belongs to me in the first place." Rage shot through her body. "You are wasting your time with me. Arrest me if you have more questions. I suggest you go interview the actors again if you want to find the real murderer." Brenda whirled on her heel and left the rose garden.

As she walked away, he replied quietly to her retreating form, just loud enough for her to hear, "I can give you one day, Brenda. One day."

She picked up her pace until she reached the back door of the bed and breakfast. Just inside, she saw Phyllis and chef Morgan turn from the window where they had been watching her wrathful entrance.

"What was that all about?" Phyllis asked.

Brenda shook her head violently and stalked down the hallway to the back stairs and continued up the stairs at a furious pace. Phyllis and Morgan turned to look at each other in consternation, then Phyllis followed her. At the top of the stairs she hesitated and then kept walking to catch up to Brenda. When Phyllis entered the farthest attic room, she found Brenda pulling stacks of papers from a large crate. Her eyes were rimmed with red but not a tear spilled on her cheeks.

"Brenda, you can trust me. Tell me what is going on."

"Mac considers me his top suspect in the murder of Ellen Teague." She bent back to the crate and yanked out another handful of papers and sorted through them quickly.

"How can he begin to think that?" Phyllis replied in shock.

"I don't know, but he does." Brenda interspersed her tale of the recent events with Mac in between sorting through the mess of papers arrayed around her. When she finished she barely suppressed the sobs that tried to bubble to the surface. She looked at the empty crates and sat back on her heels. "Help me go through all of this. Please, Phyllis. Look for anything that has Ellen Teague's name on it. I don't care if it is a ticket, a theatre bill, a letter, a legal document. Anything. There's got to be something here that can help me."

They dug in silence for a while. Brenda sputtered more words, still finding it hard to believe she found herself in this situation. "He has given me a day to solve this murder case and then he will issue a warrant for my arrest."

This time Phyllis gasped. "He's gone crazy. There are plenty of actors who arrived with Ellen who intensely disliked her. Any of them could have had a motive, but not you, Brenda. He should know better than that." She hugged Brenda. "Maybe he's just frustrated that he has no solid leads and is taking it out on you. I don't mean to excuse him for his behavior but it may explain some things."

"No one solves a murder case this complicated in two days," Brenda said. "He knows that. After all, he is the detective and I'd like to see him solve cases that fast."

Phyllis didn't say it but she figured that in Mac's mind, he had solved the case. Brenda felt rather than saw Phyllis stop what she was doing. She knew Phyllis's eyes were glued to her.

"Why does Mac see you as the prime suspect?"

"Before her death, Ellen met with Edward Graham and told him she planned to file a lawsuit against me for ownership of the bed and breakfast. She claims that Randolph promised her this place. The draft of the lawsuit Edward received stated that she had proof in New York and planned to send it immediately to Edward once she arrived back home."

"And that's all Mac has to go on?" Phyllis narrowed her eyes as she pondered this. "It seems to me that Ellen would have brought that proof with her if she had it."

Brenda flashed her housekeeper a grateful look. "I agree. But also – our guests heard me arguing with Ellen about her preposterous claims the night she was killed."

"Well, I'm still baffled. He needs to get past his suspicions once and for all. We are all behind you, Brenda. You can count on Sweetfern Harbor. I'll get Molly on it along with her friends. My daughter has a steady run of customers in Morning Sun Coffee every day. She also told me the actors often talk freely when they are there. Allie will help, and her mother will listen to her customers, too, in case she overhears something useful. Everyone goes in for goodies from Hope Williams's bakery."

Brenda began to feel better. Phyllis was right. Sweetfern Harbor was a tight-knit family and Brenda could count on support as she raced against the clock. In the meantime, she would conduct her own line of questioning with her guests. She didn't bother wasting time wondering why Mac hadn't interviewed everyone a second time before fastening onto his suspicions that her motive was the strongest. The blood rushing through her changed from livid anger to determination. She thought about Jenny Rivers, who was Mac's daughter, but also a close friend to many in the community. Brenda wondered if Jenny would take Brenda's side or the side of her detective father.

It didn't take long for word to spread among friends and Jenny called Brenda as soon as she heard, outraged at her father. "Don't worry, Brenda, I will personally help you prove him wrong. I've always been good at getting people to talk without them realizing how much they are saying." Brenda had to chuckle. Jenny did have a way of charming information from unsuspecting people while they perused the florist shop. She thanked Jenny and was relieved to feel that she had such strong support even from Mac's daughter. Brenda quickly asked Jenny what she knew about any suspicious messages delivered with flower bouquets, but the florist said it must not have come from her shop. Perhaps it had been one of the many bouquets thrown onstage at the close of the performance, and so it was impossible to tell where it had come from.

Now that the town was on her side, she focused on her guests. She had two hours before they would leave for the park to perform one last time in Sweetfern Harbor with the Seaside Theatre Festival before it toured back to

New York City. She gathered them all together and told them she wanted to speak with them again. Though it was unorthodox, she chose to have them all together. She wanted to observe their reactions to one another and to pick up any innuendo they might exchange between themselves.

"Where's Chester?" she asked, as she realized the group was short one person.

"We thought you wanted to talk with the cast only," Ricky said with surprise.

"He's a cast member now," Anna pointed out. "He's going to play the country estate host so Bonnie can take Ellen's part. I guess we forgot, we're so used to him being an assistant to..." Anna didn't seem to want to even say the late actress's name.

Shawn went upstairs to find Chester. He came down alone, shrugging his shoulders at Brenda. "He is nowhere to be found. He must have taken a walk into town."

Brenda thought perhaps it would be better to have a one-on-one with Chester, so she let it go for the moment. She told them she wanted to hear their accounts of the evening before, when everyone had returned to the bed and breakfast. She began with Bonnie, who eagerly repeated the same story she told Brenda and Mac. One by one Brenda asked the others, and they stuck to their stories.

"Did you and Anna go to sleep right around ten or so?" she asked Shawn.

"We were sound asleep as soon as our heads hit the pillows," he said. He smiled. "We woke up when we heard you yelling at Ellen." Despite the actress's death, he appeared to still see humor in the incident. "None of us ever got the last word with her like that," said Shawn. That's all it took for the rest of the group to smile, as well. Brenda was still shocked at their lack of sadness at Ellen Teague's death, and she began to wonder if perhaps all of them had planned the murder together. They were actors, after all. Perhaps they were so good at acting they were hiding their true intentions. She could only hope that repeated questions would trip them up, if so.

After an hour of questions and verifying little details, Brenda was disappointed to discover nothing out of place with any of their stories. She wished them well on the last performance. "I hope you still have a good turnout tonight."

"Oh, I think we'll have a bigger crowd than ever," said Ricky with a smirk. "The tabloids are all over Ellen's death and there's probably just as many gawkers as there are theatre fans with tickets tonight. I heard ticket scalpers are making a pretty penny down on Main Street."

As the rest of the actors turned to leave to get ready for the performance, Brenda pulled Shawn and Anna aside briefly. "I won't take long since I know you have to get ready. What can you tell me about Chester? How long did he work for Ellen?"

"I think he was with her for at least twenty years. I'm basing that on the plays he mentioned working on with her." Anna looked at Shawn. "Do you think that's about right?"

"Yes, at least twenty years." When Brenda pressed him for details about Chester's temperament, Shawn continued. "He's a nice guy. I don't think I've ever seen him get upset with anyone, not even Ellen. He seemed to take her in stride better than any of us. That's probably how he stayed in that job for so long." Anna nodded in agreement.

"Did you know that he was well acquainted with Randolph?" asked Anna. "He and Randolph knew one another quite well." Brenda expressed surprise at this unknown detail, but realized she had already taken too much of their time, and thanked them for their cooperation. They turned to hurry upstairs, their hands together as they left her. She watched as they exchanged knowing glances and she wondered what else they weren't sharing with her.

Brenda glanced at her watch. Perhaps Chester was avoiding further questions by going straight to Harbor Park from his walk into town. Brenda went back upstairs to the attic and unlocked the door. She pulled a Windsor chair from against the wall and brushed off the dust and cobwebs that covered it. Sitting down, she picked up a stack of papers she had left unsorted after her earlier attempt to find evidence with Phyllis's help. Several folders held scripts for plays. When she opened one, Randolph's lines were there in front of her, and she tried to imagine his resonant voice booming out from the stage. He had shared leading roles with Ellen Teague in most of them. From several playbills, she could see that he had also directed quite a few. She picked up the third folder and noticed a bundle of letters under it. The letter on top was written in a distinct, old-fashioned handwriting and addressed to Randolph Sheffield. The precise script seemed familiar to her but she could not place it.

Brenda examined the letter and found it was still sealed. Could humid conditions have caused its glue to reseal? She inspected it closely and determined there was no way this letter had been read. Carefully opening it, she scanned down for the signature. To her great surprise, she read Chester Boyd's name signed under the phrase 'Your great admirer and good friend.'

It was dated just a few months before her uncle's death. She wondered why it hadn't been opened. Brenda read the letter with growing curiosity.

Dear Randolph,

I can't tell you how excited I am to be coming to Sheffield Bed and Breakfast with the Seaside Theatre Festival next year. I've waited a long time to see what you left the theatre for and now I'll have my chance. Ellen has the cast lined up for "The Rich Game" and I know it will be a hit. Best of all, I will be playing a role in it for the first time. My dreams of acting are finally becoming reality. We aren't getting any younger, Randolph, as we both know, and this has been my lifelong dream. This may well be my last chance. I realize working next to Ellen won't hurt my chances either.

I am happy that Sweetfern Harbor will host the theatre festival. It will be just like old times! I can't thank you enough for telling me to never give up on my dreams. I may not be as talented as you, but I am lucky to count myself as your friend. I must study my lines now and so will close off.

Your great admirer and good friend,

Chester

Brenda looked at the dates again. Remorse hit her that her uncle wasn't there to see his friends perform in his beloved town of Sweetfern Harbor. But oddly enough, Chester was so sure he had a part in the play and yet he had arrived as Ellen's assistant. What had happened in between this letter and their arrival?

There was one person who might be able to answer Brenda's questions and that was William Pendleton. As a lifelong resident and a staunch promoter of the arts, he would no doubt know something about how her Uncle Randolph had helped play a part in bringing the theatre festival to town. She recalled how at ease he was with Ellen the night after the play when they shared champagne together in her suite.

Brenda searched for Phyllis and found her dusting in the sitting room. "Do you know if William plans to attend the final night of the play tonight?"

"He decided he didn't want to go, out of respect for Ellen's death. He is quite upset. He was a great admirer of hers." Brenda asked if he was home. "He's at home until this evening. We have plans to have a nice dinner out since the cast will be leaving."

"I suppose Mac told them they could all leave right away?"

Phyllis glanced down at the duster in her hand. "We all know he is wrong about you, Brenda. Once he lets them all leave he will be sorry he did that. They will go on to the next city for their next play and he will have a hard time getting them all corralled again."

But Brenda simply said, "I can be reached at the Pendleton home if needed." She had no time to lose, and immediately left to drive to William's house, her thoughts racing.

CHAPTER EIGHT

SWITCHED ROLES

renda's car wound its way up the tree-lined driveway to the Pendleton home and she idly wondered how many workers it took to maintain the beautiful gardens and the sprawling manicured lawn. The more modest grounds of the Sheffield Bed and Breakfast were under the care of a father and son team who took care of many other business properties in Brenda's neighborhood. Surely this would require a small army of arborists and landscapers, however.

William answered the door and invited her inside. They sat in leather chairs that flanked a massive stone fireplace in the luxuriously appointed living room. He offered her something to drink and she declined. She questioned him about his visit to Ellen's room the night before her death, and his eyes immediately misted over.

"Ellen's death is a true tragedy." He dabbed at the corner of one eye with a linen pocket square. "But I must admit, it's equally sad that your Uncle Randolph missed out on seeing the Seaside Theatre Festival here. The theatre was his life and he never left it for good, even in his retirement."

Brenda smiled. "I had no idea until recently that he was ever in show business."

"Oh yes, he was an actor for nearly ten years and then directed several very successful plays. I'm surprised your family didn't know that about him."

"Theatre may be the reason why my father never talked about him. My father believed in going to a good job day in and day out and making a steady, decent living. I'm beginning to think he didn't approve of his brother's choice of career, no matter how successful Randolph was." But as she said this, she reflected on the enigma of their relationship, since the letter indicated the two brothers were closer than she had suspected. Randolph spilled his feelings to his brother. That said something.

"That's too bad. Randolph's talent showed in everything he put his finger on." William looked her in the eye. "Now what brings you here to see me?"

"How well do you know Chester Boyd?"

"Ellen's assistant? I know him well enough, though I've never considered him a close friend. He was very good to

Ellen and put up with a lot from her. She was very demanding, which explains why he always appeared so prim and proper. His was a privileged life, to be that close to someone as famous in Hollywood and the theatre world as she was."

The air seemed suspended for a few seconds. Brenda knew more was coming.

"There's one thing I've never figured out, though. Chester was originally cast in 'The Rich Game' as I recall. I helped the festival with the local publicity. Chester called to confirm the final cast list to be printed on the playbills and the posters and I was surprised to see his name there as well, and congratulated him. I had already ordered the posters when a few hours later he called back to say he had been mistaken. He wasn't going to be in it after all." He chuckled ruefully at the memory. "I had to hurry up and correct the order. His name was gone and Bonnie Ross was listed instead. He never explained what happened and he seemed embarrassed by the whole thing."

"Do you know what role he was supposed to play?"

"I'm not sure of that since the posters listed the actors and not their parts. The exception was Ellen and Ricky Owens, who played her husband. Their names were printed with their photos and roles."

Brenda absorbed this information and cast her mind

about, still not sure what to make of it. "Do you have a take on who may have murdered Ellen?"

William looked taken aback, but looked at her directly with a sympathetic look. "I know you didn't do it. You are much like your uncle when it comes to having a gentle personality. I can't see you strangling Ellen with her belt." He smiled. "In answer to your question, I do know that most, if not all, of the actors disliked her. I liked her dearly as a friend, but she was a hard woman to work under. But I haven't the faintest idea who might hold a grudge so severe as to kill the woman."

Brenda thanked William Pendleton for the information he gave her. She didn't feel she could fully rule William out, but nothing really indicated he had anything to do with it. Back in her car she reflected on the detail of the sudden change in casting, and realized she didn't know much about Bonnie Ross. Every other actor might have disliked Ellen, but no one else's casting had changed. Only Bonnie was a newcomer.

It was already early evening and the summer sky was a brilliant dark blue as the stars began to appear. Brenda decided to drive by Harbor Park. The performance was due to end in half an hour, which would give her time to observe the actors from a distance. Tonight, after this performance, would be her last chance to talk to the actors before they left town, and then her time would be up, and Mac would come to find her.

She stood under the large oak tree at the edge of the park and watched the stage. She picked up enough of the flow of words between the actors to follow the comical scene. When Chester Boyd spoke his lines, he was truly amazing. His diction was perfect and he knew the part well. The audience loved him and he seemed a natural on stage. It had to have been a practiced role. She was disappointed that she hadn't been early enough to catch any of the major scenes with Bonnie in Ellen's old role. She wondered how well Bonnie knew Ellen. With Ellen's penchant for manipulation, had she cast Bonnie to butter her up for some reason? Or had the casting change been merely to spite Chester?

The cast received a standing ovation at the end. There was no Ellen Teague to push to the front as they exited a side door into the waiting crowd. Instead, all of the actors were mobbed by autograph hounds and photographers. As Brenda watched, broad grins spread across every face as they scribbled their names and best wishes onto the photographs and playbills thrust in their faces. A few reporters even pressed the actors for quotes on Ellen's death as photographers clicked away, but they all declined to comment. All in all, it took a long while before the crowd died down and left. Brenda walked forward and congratulated the actors for a job well done.

"It means a lot that we could be here and stay at the Sheffield and reminisce about your uncle," said Shawn.

"He never let us forget how important the arts are, even in small towns."

Anna's eyes held joy but also great sympathy. "We hoped he would pull through his illness and be here to see the Seaside Theatre Festival. It would have been like a reunion."

Brenda realized that this tight-knit group of actors was her uncle's adopted family, just as Sweetfern Harbor had become to him later. She looked at the happy faces surrounding her and felt a crushing sense of loss at the idea that she might lose the Sheffield Bed and Breakfast and her uncle's legacy. She wordlessly watched the cast members as they chatted under the starry skies.

Bonnie's face practically glowed as the others heaped praises on her performance in Ellen's former role. As she chatted with Chester about how privileged she felt despite Ellen's death, Brenda was surprised again by how different Chester's face was now. Instead of his usual stony expression, he relaxed and laughed along with the others, just as he had in his role on the stage, in a way Brenda would never have thought possible for the previously stoic and proper assistant.

Ricky Owens came to Brenda's side and asked to speak privately with her. They stopped near the oak tree where Brenda had stood watching the play while the others continued to chat.

"What is it?"

"Word has spread that you are suspected of murdering Ellen," he said. "I want you to know that none of us believe you had anything to do with it. Everyone argued with Ellen when she got to be too much. I mean everyone – except Chester and maybe Bonnie. That woman was not easy to get along with."

Brenda's smile didn't reach her eyes. Aside from the sad fact that suspicions had spread through the rumor mill, she was also worried that everyone except Mac seemed to be ready to reassure her. Not to mention the fact that she hadn't been able to turn up a shred of evidence pointing to any other suspect. Dread washed over her and she realized how precarious her reputation was. If word spread that she was the prime suspect then everyone would hate her for killing the famous star. The blood drained from her cheeks as she pictured her face splashed across the tabloids and she thanked her lucky stars that no reporters had approached her about the rumors so far.

Ricky noticed the sudden change in her demeanor. "We know you're innocent," said Ricky. He repeated it twice more. "I'm sure the real killer will be found and you will be vindicated."

If the killer is found soon, thought Brenda. The clock was ticking down fast.

"Do you have any idea who did it?" Ricky looked away

when she asked the question and she could see again the hint of something unsaid on his face. "Please, Ricky, whatever you say will stay right here between us. I just need a lead to figure out who had a motive. My reputation is at stake – and my freedom."

He paused, as if reluctant to admit that he knew something that could help her. He turned and met the pleading look in her eyes and finally gave in. "I'll tell you one thing, but you didn't hear it from me. It's about Bonnie."

Brenda took a step closer to him and blinked in disbelief. "Bonnie? What could she possibly have to do with Ellen's death?"

"She is Ellen's niece. But she would never boast about it. Ellen has been estranged from her entire family for many years, she claims she cut them off but I'm not sure...it might have been the other way around. Anyway, Bonnie pestered her for auditions for years, ever since she was fifteen or so. Ellen finally cast her, but I think there was something going on under the surface."

Brenda attempted to wrap her head around the fact that Bonnie Ross was Ellen Teague's niece. She thought back to her interviews with Bonnie and racked her mind for any detail that stood out, but nothing came to mind. Ricky continued his story.

"I overheard Ellen on the phone once with her estranged

sister, Bonnie's mother. She said this was the last straw, and Bonnie had pushed her luck far enough. I got the impression that Bonnie realized soon after that that she had no hope of future support from Ellen."

Brenda was intrigued. "That does shed a new light on things...but I need to bring hard evidence to the police, not speculation."

"I'm sorry I don't have anything more. But it did bother me that you didn't know the backstory about Bonnie and I'm glad to get it off my chest. Maybe it can help in some way."

"Thanks for telling me this." She congratulated him again and they parted ways.

Brenda sat in her car afterward and thought about Ricky's words. She watched the actors as they walked through the park and headed toward Sheffield Bed and Breakfast. Mac is making a mistake allowing them to leave town, she thought bitterly. She knew that most of them had already packed up and only had a few details to take care of back at the bed and breakfast. In less than three hours they would be on the road again. Time was of the essence for Brenda, so she wasted no time in driving back home.

Chef Morgan was busy preparing a light dinner when Brenda walked in. She helped Phyllis carry trays of drinks into the sitting room where the actors would gather before they departed the bed and breakfast. When Brenda entered the front hall, she found Bonnie talking with Allie. As usual, Bonnie was in a jovial mood, talking animatedly with the young employee. Brenda greeted both of them and then asked Bonnie to join her in the office in back of the reception desk. When they settled down in comfortable chairs, Brenda got right to the point.

"I didn't get to see the whole show this afternoon but I heard you performed your new part well, even with such short notice. Congratulations are in order. I'm curious...I never asked you about how you got cast under Ellen Teague?"

The young actress gave her a winning smile and tucked a lock of hair behind one ear. "I worked for it. I took acting classes and I begged Ellen more than once to give me a part. I didn't care if it was just a small one. I've always wanted to act. She finally caved in and gave me an audition, and I got the part of the hostess of the country estate. It was my big break as far as I was concerned."

Brenda eyed the vivacious young woman in the chair before her. Nothing seemed false about her, but Brenda got the impression that she was seeing a façade. "Did you know Ellen for long?" Ah, that got a response. Bonnie cast her eyes down at her lap and her long lashes seemed to tremble as if she was about to cry.

"To tell you the truth, Ellen Teague was my aunt, though I was sworn to secrecy about that. I can't believe she's gone." She brushed a tear away from the corner of her eye and looked back up at Brenda. "Ellen had no love for her extended family and that included her own sister, my mother. I know Ellen didn't think I had much talent, but I figured if she gave me any part at all I would have a solid foundation for future work." She shrugged her shoulders prettily. "I feel...sad about Ellen's death, but not grief, if that makes sense. We had been estranged for so long and it seemed she barely tolerated me. I know that sounds cruel, but I just can't muster up grief over it at all." She looked at Brenda apologetically. "I don't mean her manner of death doesn't give me a twinge of regret. No one should have to die like that." She shuddered.

Brenda made a mental note of her choice of words. Right now, she had more important issues to cover with Bonnie.

"Back to your audition...I understand you got it at the last minute? What happened to the person who was first assigned to your role?"

Her expression grew pensive. "You know, I never thought about that. Ellen called me instead of me calling her for a change. I was so excited that I didn't even consider who may have backed out. She told me the role came up and she would give me an audition immediately. Everything was hurried along and I was given the part the next day."

"Did you know that Chester had been promised a role in 'The Rich Game?'"

Her eyes widened and her mouth gaped open. "Really? I had no idea Chester was an actor. Though I have to admit he was great in my former role today. He has seen the play enough times to know everyone's lines." Bonnie chattered on about the performance and seemed oblivious to anything else.

Brenda dismissed the young actress from her office and sat thinking carefully through what she had heard. She realized that Bonnie Ross, for all her emotional mannerisms, was innocent. It was the image of Chester Boyd that nagged at her. Something about the man left puzzle pieces of this murder scattered and unconnected. Brenda knew all too well that time was running out for her and she had to make her next move. Instead, she was tempted to call Mac just to hear his endearing voice. They hadn't spoken since the encounter in the backyard and her heart thumped painfully in her chest to recall that moment.

"He's just waiting for me to fail so he can make an arrest." Brenda realized she was muttering out loud when Allie looked at her in a strange way. Brenda blushed. The young girl gave her a sympathetic look.

"My mother has been throwing out theories about who could have killed Ellen," Allie said. "It seems the crowds stuck around to hear more gossip about the murder, which means business at the bakery has picked up considerably. You know how my mother is. Once she's on a mission, she plans to get to the bottom of things. She's personally handing out samples to each customer just to strike up conversations with them."

Brenda smiled gratefully. "I must go down to Sweet Treats first thing tomorrow morning and thank her for her help. Has she picked up on anything helpful?"

"She just told me that Chester Boyd has been roaming around on Main Street more than the others. I think she looks at him as someone different from the other actors. He doesn't hang out with them. He is sort of aloof, don't you think so?"

Brenda absorbed this, lost in thought. One more chat with Chester Boyd was in order. She shuddered thinking she could sit in a jail cell the rest of her life while wondering if he had been the murderer. His room connected with Ellen's and so he certainly had access and opportunity. Ellen had yanked his coveted role out from underneath him and that was motive enough. He expressed in his letter to Randolph that this could be his last chance to be an actor. And then she still wondered about Anna and Shawn Quincy who often shared soft and sometimes unspoken secrets with one another. Was it more than the usual exchanges between a husband and wife? Anna had also admitted she argued with Ellen before the play. Frustrated, Brenda realized she had to go with the one scrap of physical proof she had uncovered.

Brenda hurried to the attic and retrieved the letter from

Chester to Randolph, and stuffed it in her pocket. On her way to the front door, she passed the sitting room and noticed Anna and Shawn huddled together speaking in low voices. Anna looked up and waved. Brenda greeted them and went on her way. Then she changed her mind and went into the room. Both actors looked up expectantly.

"I don't mean to intrude, but have either of you heard anything more that could lead to who committed the murder?"

They exchanged glances and then shook their heads. "We don't have any idea at all," Shawn said. "I do wish we hadn't fallen asleep so easily that night. We both slept again after hearing you and Ellen arguing. Our room is close enough to have heard something but we didn't."

Brenda didn't want to be reminded yet again of the shouting she had sunk to that night. She thanked them and told them she would be back in time to tell them all goodbye.

She yearned to call Mac and get his input on her next plan. Once again, she recalled their last visit under the rose arbor and fought to hold her tears at bay.

Instead, she called Police Chief Bob Ingram.

CHAPTER NINE

CONFESSION

Brenda looked through the window at the reporters on the sidewalk outside under the late summer evening stars. She would be thankful when the drama surrounding her was over. The reporters had hung around the bed and breakfast in ever-increasing numbers ever since Ellen Teague had been found dead in her suite.

Phyllis came up behind her. "I wish those reporters would leave. I'd like to see things back to normal around here."

"I'd like that, too," said Brenda. "I think we won't have to put up with all the chaos around here much longer."

"Surely you aren't expecting to go to jail." The housekeeper's eyes widened.

"I don't think that will happen. I hope not."

Phyllis looked beyond Brenda. "I wonder what they're up to." Brenda followed her eyes to see several police cars pulling into the driveway.

She excused herself when the chief stepped out of his patrol car in front of the bed and breakfast. The reporters all knew something big was about to happen and swarmed forward as if meshed into one big glob of humanity. Chief Ingram scanned the yard and spotted Brenda waving to him from the side door. The chief waited for another officer to get out of his car and then gave orders to the officers that followed him. They immediately pushed the reporters back to the edge of the property. From where she stood, Brenda knew Mac was with Bob Ingram, though she couldn't see him yet.

Her attention was diverted to Chester Boyd as he stepped out of the front door to the waiting limousine in the driveway. He was carrying a trunk of costumes, and behind him Shawn and Ricky came carrying several cases of props and makeup. She hurried out to them. Chief Ingram and the detective followed her. She got to the actors first, hoping that Mac wouldn't dare arrest her in front of the gathered crowd of photographers.

"Chester, I want to speak with you one last time."

When they were apart from the others, Brenda asked him about his exciting last-minute role on the stage, asking him if he had always wanted to be an actor. She noticed the two policemen waited a few yards away from them.

"I never wanted to act. I enjoy helping with the props and costumes. As Ellen's assistant, I keep...I kept things in order for everyone else." He entwined his fingers together and stood patiently and politely as they spoke. "Your bed and breakfast provided very comfortable lodgings for all of us. It's such a shame and a tragedy about Ellen's sudden death. I do hope it doesn't mar the reputation of the establishment."

"Never mind that," said Brenda, incensed at his lies. "I know you have always aspired to be an actor, Chester. I know because you were good friends with my uncle."

He shifted his stance slightly. "I don't know where you got your information, but none of it is true. I did know and admire Randolph. That part I don't dispute, but I never had aspirations to be an actor. Besides, Ellen paid me very well to assist her." He pursed his lips and made as if to rejoin the others loading the limousine.

"But it wasn't enough, was it Chester? You were at her beck and call night and day. She didn't appreciate your talents. Then when she finally gave you a part, she ripped it away from you before you could taste success." Brenda reached in her pocket and drew out the letter. She read it word for word to Chester. Anger flared across his face as he listened. She looked up at him again accusingly. "This is the same handwriting found on the threatening note in the rose bouquet next to Ellen's bed after she was killed," said Brenda.

"All right, I did want to be an actor." She noted that he had slipped right past the issue of the card in the bouquet. "I studied every speaking part and knew how a good actor sells their emotions to an audience." The resentment seemed to come off him in waves. "I had talent that superseded some of her actors and Ellen knew that. And then...and then she—"

Brenda held up her hand. "Don't you want the cops to hear you?" He gave her a furious, wordless look. But they both knew it was time for the truth to come out. Inexplicably, relief seemed to spread through him and he sighed. The police chief, accompanied by the detective, approached closer. Brenda ignored both and turned once again to Chester. She had just a few minutes to work a confession out of him or she would be arrested.

"And then what? What did Ellen do?"

The normally sedate man's eyes darted from Brenda to the police standing there and then back to her.

"The letter only tells half the story. She approached me in New York last year during casting. Ellen told me if I wanted to play the role of the host of the country estate in 'The Rich Game' that it was mine. She said it was time for my talents to be recognized. She assured me the role was mine." He paused and his eyes darkened with remembered anger, like bright flames in his pupils. "She promised it to me. I even called William Pendleton to tell him to add my name to the billboard posters. He was doing the promotion for us down here. But I could tell she didn't like the thought of me getting above my station," he said sourly. "The next thing I knew, Ellen came to me and announced she had given the role to someone else. I don't hold any grudges against Bonnie, but that part was meant to be mine. As usual, Ellen relished the power that she had to give and to snatch away at whim. Ask anyone. You saw for yourself what she was like during that ghastly final rehearsal. Her reasons were never understood by any of us, but she didn't care."

Mac started to step forward. Brenda reached her arm out and stopped him. She did not look at him. This was her game and her life at stake. Detective Mac Rivers wasn't going to have the privilege of sharing her limelight just now.

"Tell me what happened." Brenda had patience. "I can see your predicament. She upstaged everyone and cheated the cast out of their well-deserved acclamations. You merited recognition, too, Chester. You waited on her hand and foot. I'm sure you never had a minute you could call your own. And then she took your part away."

Chester looked at Brenda and it was as if they were speaking alone on the quiet stairway landing once more, and not in front of the police and the distant hubbub of the reporters. At last, things could be said once and for all. He was ready to clear the air. "Ellen Teague was selfish. She was a tyrant." He practically spit the words out. "She was never happy unless everyone's attention focused on her. Randolph Sheffield was the best man and best actor I've ever known and Ellen used him like she did everyone else. I know why your uncle left the theatre. He was sick of Ellen Teague. Randolph was the most talented man I've known but she crushed him under her heel again and again. That's why he left, even though theatre was in his life's blood."

Brenda saw the pain written on Chester's face. "I read a letter Uncle Randolph wrote to my father. In it he said he had had enough of Ellen." She hoped he had more to say, and waited, holding her breath.

"I waited on that woman for twenty years. I can count on one hand the times she said thank you for anything I did. I got her out of more than one crisis when it came to producing plays. I'm ashamed to say I begged her for a role every year when a new play came out or an actor left a role at the last minute. She knew my ambitions. And she told me I was where she wanted me. That was well put. She had me where she wanted me and I was crazy to think I would be anything different than her servant."

The two officers remained where Brenda told them to stand. Brenda knew the reporters at the edge of the property were getting impatient, but this had to be done right. The press would have to wait.

"The biggest privilege of my life would have been to act on stage under the direction of Randolph Sheffield. Ellen knew of our friendship and couldn't stand it. She made sure I was so busy there was no time to even audition for Randolph, and then later she threw it in my face that he never would have cast me." He heaved an angry sigh at the memory. "And then...when she finally told me I was cast in this play, she took it away without a second thought and gave it to an unknown." His eyes closed momentarily and a muscle twitched in his jaw.

"And you knew then that your dream would never be realized under Ellen Teague," Brenda finished.

"Randolph knew when it was time to go. That was one of the great tragedies for the world of theatre, his retirement from the stage. I never forgave her for that. But when she took the role from me, I finally had enough of her, too." He looked directly at Brenda. "There's one more thing I must tell you. Your uncle did have one short conversation with Ellen about the bed and breakfast. It was when he told her his plans of moving to Sweetfern Harbor. He never once promised her she would one day own it – in fact, she mocked him for his choice to move to such a tiny town. But after he left, she laughed about it and told me she would one day get her hands on the property just to spite Randolph and any family he had."

Now they were getting someplace. She mentally willed the officers to stay where they were. This saga wasn't over yet. Chester focused on Brenda and smiled wearily.

"The performance this afternoon was my triumph over Ellen Teague. It was the happiest moment of my life and I wouldn't change it for anything. I did everyone a service that night." Chester Boyd chuckled as if they were simply having a normal conversation. "It was so easy. There she was, almost passed out from the champagne. Her dressing gown was on the brass hook next to her bed with the belt dangling. It was all so easy. I took my time and she didn't even know what I was doing. I even fingered the belt and then got it ready." Chester did not take his eyes off Brenda's as he said these words and a deadly chill raced through her as she glimpsed the darkness inside him. "One strong pull was all it took and I kept it tight on her until she was dead."

Brenda stepped back in fearful triumph, her heart pounding, and Detective Mac Rivers snapped handcuffs on the actor's wrists and read him his rights. Brenda shakily thanked Chester for the truth and turned to watch as Mac escorted Chester through the group of actors gathered outside on the way to the patrol car.

"Break a leg, guys," he said with ghastly calm. "Never forget you are great actors." He and Bonnie exchanged glances. He smiled at her gently. "You especially, Bonnie, don't give up on your dreams." He ducked his head and was quickly settled in the backseat of the squad car.

Brenda was torn between feeling relief and shock at how everything had turned out. She watched the strange scene on the driveway as cameras flashed in the darkness from the photographers gathered some distance away. Now that the truth had been revealed, it seemed as if the actors felt free to express themselves without reservation. Shawn and Anna both mouthed a silent "Thank you" to Chester through the window. Bonnie allowed tears to stream down her cheeks. Ricky nodded as if silently paying his respects to Chester's terrible act. They were all thanking the man for killing the woman they hated.

Brenda watched Chester Boyd's reaction, too. His mouth curved upward in a small smile as he was driven to the police station to be booked for murder. His dream of becoming an actor on the stage, though short-lived, had been fulfilled. Brenda reflected that perhaps his final speech to her on the driveway had been a performance, too. It was his story, the last story he would get to tell, after all.

CHAPTER TEN

RECONCILIATION

*D*etective Mac Rivers finished speaking to the chief as they stood together in front of the Sheffield Bed and Breakfast. He told the chief he would be back at the police station soon. He glanced at the last of the reporters who turned to leave as the scene was now quiet. Under the summer stars, he walked toward the edge of the lawn to gaze down at the ocean as it lapped gently on the rocks a short distance below. He had his work cut out for him. Following leads in a murder case was minuscule compared to facing Brenda Sheffield. He sat on a bench that faced the view and watched the waves lapping against the rocks. He still clutched the warrant for Brenda's arrest in his right hand. He smoothed it out on his knee and then methodically tore it into tiny bits. The wind carried the scraps of paper over the ocean until most dropped into the water while the rest of the pieces stayed with the wind. He hoped he had not lost Brenda forever over his stupid assumptions. She was right when she told him he didn't know her at all. He had made a mistake, but he knew he loved her.

———

Brenda and Phyllis went upstairs to the guest rooms. Without words, both women ripped the yellow tape from around the suite Ellen stayed in.

"What about the tape around Chester's room?"

"Rip it off, too, Phyllis."

"Have the police got all the evidence they need from this room?"

Brenda shrugged her shoulders. "They've spent enough time in and around these two rooms. I think they have all they need. Rip it off."

Phyllis did as she was told, relieved the nightmare was over. Brenda helped her strip the beds. Without words, she took the bedding to the dumpster and threw it away. On her way back through the kitchen door, Chef Morgan called to her.

"The detective is looking for you."

Brenda sighed. "He'll just have to find me on his own. I have a bed and breakfast to get back in order."

Morgan watched Brenda stop to wash her hands in the sink. "That man is in love with you, you know. This old house can wait," she said gently. She could see the pain in Brenda's eyes but her boss said nothing as she dried her hands and turned to get back to work.

"I've been looking for you."

Brenda was halfway up the stairs when she heard his voice. Her heart lurched. She turned to see him standing at the bottom of the staircase.

"Did you need something? I presumed you had everything you needed by now."

"Not everything." He shifted from one foot to the other. "I want to talk with you privately."

Brenda debated within herself. She decided he should wonder a little longer about whether she would let him make amends or not. Her heart still hurt, though she could feel it thawing in his presence. "I'll be free in about an hour or so. We have guests coming in early tomorrow morning and everyone is behind on duties right now."

Mac knew that was all he was going to get for the moment. "I'll be back. Maybe we can go down to the ocean and enjoy the breezes and a cocktail?"

"That sounds good if I can get done with everything in

time." Brenda turned from him and ascended the steps. She smiled with a certain satisfaction. Perhaps she was giving him the same uncaring treatment he had given her, but she didn't look back.

"Did I hear Mac's voice?" Phyllis asked her upstairs, hoping he and Brenda patched up their differences. If they didn't, Sweetfern Harbor and Sheffield Bed and Breakfast would have two very unhappy residents.

"He wants to see me when I have time."

Phyllis looked at her in slight exasperation. "You have time right now. I can handle the rest of this. Allie will help me catch up. She already got rid of all the flowers that were up here."

Brenda grinned. "I think it's good if he stews for another hour or so, don't you?"

Phyllis waved her dust cloth at Brenda. "Don't put him on hold too long," she said. "But, yes, it probably won't hurt him." Both women laughed at their joke as they continued to work side by side.

It wasn't much longer when she and Phyllis had finished readying most of the rooms. The housekeeper suggested she leave to find Mac, but emotions battled within Brenda. Finally she shrugged helplessly. "What can I say? I'm in love with the man." Phyllis gave her a thumbs-up and grinned when Brenda pulled her cell phone from her pocket.

"Hello, Brenda." She could hear Mac's breathing was a little fast when he answered her. It made her feel warm just like always.

"I'll meet you down at our spot on the waterfront in fifteen minutes." She hung up.

He realized he had no idea what she meant, but he felt a twinge of joy at the way her voice changed from the cold tone earlier to lukewarm. He told the police chief he had some business to take care of. "I should be back in a little while."

Bob grinned at him. "It's about time you got your head on straight again, Mac. Take the rest of the night off. Chester Boyd isn't going anywhere. His arraignment is scheduled for tomorrow morning." He bent to the paperwork on his desk and waved the detective away.

Mac let his memory guide him to the café where they had met for dinner just a few short days ago. He caught a glimpse of her gleaming auburn hair swaying slightly in the ocean breeze as she stood under a streetlight. She wore a light-pink cotton skirt that reached her ankles and showed off perfectly manicured toes in espadrille sandals. A gauzy shirt in a darker shade of pink completed her look. Their eyes met and both walked toward each other. He grasped her hand in his and without speaking they strolled toward the edge of the water. Neither seemed ready to talk just yet. Mac led her to a secluded spot. Brenda recognized it as the place they chose when they enjoyed their first real date together. In spite of the stunning view before them, both of them thought about the recent events.

"You know, Mac, fame can do strange things to people. I found that out this weekend. All the actors wanted attention and adulation from fans, Ellen Teague more than anyone. So much so, that it turned her into a narcissistic and selfish person." She paused. "I can understand how she drove Chester to his breaking point."

"Circumstances can do that to some people. This week turned me into someone I didn't recognize either, Brenda." He looked into her eyes and she read the sincerity written there.

Her warm smile turned into a half-grin, and it drew him toward her. He pulled her down next to him on a rock where they had an expansive view of the crashing ocean waves. The moonlight left glittering diamonds scattered across the waters. Brenda leaned into Mac's strong arms, enjoying the moment. He released her and stood up. She was reluctant to let go of the warmth that flooded through her at his touch.

"Don't get up, Brenda. I want to look at you when I tell you how sorry I am that I judged you so harshly. I should have known you are not capable of any kind of violence, much less murder. I know you would have fought it out in court to make sure you kept ownership of the bed and breakfast. I was so wrong. I am sorry and I hope you find it in your heart to forgive me for being so heartless and stupid." He searched her face.

"I forgive you, Mac. I admit I was very hurt. I understood how frustrating this case was. I wished we could have worked together through the end of it. There were too many possibilities of who could have committed the crime. If I hadn't found Uncle Randolph's letter from Chester, I'm not sure how I would have extracted his confession." She smiled. "You are forgiven. Let's not talk of it again. We both made mistakes with one another and I hope we never go down that road again."

Mac beamed and she smiled back with all the love in her heart. Then he knelt down on one knee in the deep sand, reached into his pocket and brought out a velvet box. He opened it for Brenda to look inside.

"That's not the promise ring," she said in confusion. She gaped at the sparkling jewel inside.

"We are beyond promise rings," he replied. "Will you marry me, Brenda Sheffield?"

She wanted to say something memorable in response, but was speechless. Instead, she nodded her head vigorously to tell him yes. He laughed and slipped the elegant diamond ring onto her finger.

Mac swept her into his arms and kissed her. Brenda melted into his embrace. She had everything: her bed and breakfast, a town filled with people she considered family, and now Mac Rivers. Words finally came back to her. She leaned back from his lips and looked up at him.

"I'm the happiest woman in Sweetfern Harbor."

He enfolded her in his arms again and found it impossible to let go for a long, long time.

ABOUT THE AUTHOR

Wendy Meadows is an emerging author of cozy mysteries. She lives in "The Granite State" with her husband, two sons, two cats and lovable Labradoodle.

When she isn't working on her stories she likes to tend to her flower garden, relax with adult coloring and play video games with her family.

Get in Touch with Wendy

www.wendymeadows.com
wendy@wendymeadows.com